MW00884246

THE MERE TREATY

KEEPER OF DRAGONS

BOOK 3

J.A. Culican

Copyright © 2017 by J.A. Culican

All Rights Reserved.

No part of this book may be reproduced in any form or by any electronic or mechanical means, including information storage and retrieval systems, without the express written consent from the author, except in the case of a reviewer, who may quote brief passages embodied in critical articles or in a review. Trademark names appear throughout this book. Rather than trademark name, names are used in an editorial fashion, with no intention of infringement of the respective owner's trademark.

The information in this book is distributed on an "as is" basis, without warranty. Although every precaution has been taken in preparation of this work, neither the author nor the publisher shall have any liability to any person or entity with respect to any loss or damage caused or alleged to be caused directly or indirectly by the information contained in this book.

The characters, locations, and events portrayed in this book are fictitious. Any similarities or resemblance to real persons, living or dead is coincidental and not intended by the author.

Edited by: Cassidy Taylor

Cover Art by: Christian Bentulan

ISBN: 978-1979861700

www.dragonrealmpress.com

For Annabella, may you continue to grow-up strong and fearless.

Contents

Prologue

Sixty-seven minutes. That's how long it had been since Eldrick won. Not just won, but demolished us. Gaber hadn't moved from the spot we found him in and no one had said a word. Reality of the events hadn't kicked in yet, or maybe I was just in shock.

I finally found my feet and wandered a few yards away to an old tree stump. My whole body ached, and not just physically. My heart was broken. All the Elves and Trolls that we'd left behind were gone, kidnapped by the Elden. My head spun with all the possibilities of their fate. A fate they entrusted to me.

A loud clanking sound met my ears as a large shadow enveloped me. My heart jumped when my eyes met Jericho's.

"You need to stay close, my prince." He growled and tilted his head to the ground beside him.

On the snow-covered dirt lay an old sword enclosed in a brown leather sheath. The thin handle glinted at me even though the sun had stopped shining on our home that once seemed like paradise. The sword beckoned me as I grabbed the hilt and pulled it from its cover. It was lighter than I had expected as I held it out in front of me.

"This is not a toy." Jericho grabbed the sword from my hand. "Weaponry is the last level of training, but given the circumstances, it is imperative that we skip some lessons and start your training immediately."

Was he really discussing training with me right now? We just lost.

"A dragon's sword is a part of him." He leaned down and sheathed the sword. "Always keep it attached to your back. You will learn to use your mahier to keep it close even when shifted into your dragon."

Jericho dropped the sword into my lap and I wrapped my hand around the soft leather. "Why would a dragon need a sword?" I asked. I mean, dragons had fire and could fly. Why would we fight with swords?

"These battles you have fought have been nothing more than a path to war. In a war, it is vital to keep your mahier strong. When you shift, you use your mahier. When you breathe fire, you use your mahier. Your sword uses none. It is always available while keeping your mahier full." The more Jericho spoke, the brighter his eyes shone. "You are the Keeper of Dragons. A time of fear is upon us. The fate of all True beings is in your hands. Keep them strong."

I attached the sword to my back, pulling the leather straps tight around my chest. With each breath I took, I felt the sword shift on my back and the straps dig into my upper body. Jericho was right. For some reason, Eva and I were chosen by the Fates to be the Keeper of Dragons. It has been our destiny since the day we were born.

My eyes scanned the other creatures as they slowly began to come back to reality. Cairo was almost glued to Eva's side. Tears ran down her cheeks, but he had his arm around her shoulder as he whispered words of encouragement in her ear. Evander found his feet and helped Gaber to stand. His body shook as he blew out a harsh breath. His once bright eyes looked dull, as if his internal light had been extinguished. Slowly, Evander, King of the Trolls, escorted Prince Gaber toward one of the walkways.

"Keeper of Dragons." Queen Annabelle of the Fairies' voice made me jump. "Please keep me informed of any developments. The Elven Alliance is still in effect. But I must return home to check on my remaining Fairies. It seems the few that remained have been scared off."

I nodded my agreement, unable to find the words. I was scared, too.

"You defeated the Farro tonight. For that, we will forever be grateful." My eyes met hers as a sad smile formed on her face. "They are alive. I feel it within me. We will find them. And you, Keeper of Dragons, will save us all." With that, she turned her back to me and took off into the evening sky.

Both Jericho and I watched Queen Annabelle and the few remaining Fairies until they were nothing more than spots in the sky. The weight of her words held me in place. The Fairies placed their fate in me even after we lost to King Eldrick.

Jericho put his hand on my shoulder, pulling me from my thoughts. "Meet in the command center in an hour. We must prepare for war." He growled and stomped off toward Cairo and Eva.

War. A war solely on my shoulders.

J.A. Culican

Chapter One

I stood on the steps of Ochana Castle, Sila and Rylan behind me to either side, and stared out over the sea of dragon faces. They all stared up at me with pleading, adoring eyes, chanting at me to save them. Save their families. Save their homes.

From behind, Sila whispered in my ear, "We have faith in you, Son. You are the Keeper of Dragons. For you, everything is possible. I know you can do it."

They were all wrong. I shook my head and tried to tell them I was just a boy. Okay, so maybe I was eighteen, but that was barely an adult in human terms, and I was almost a baby to the dragons. "I—"

The roar from the audience was so loud that it drowned out even my own voice. How could Sila's whisper have reached me over the crowd? I needed to make everyone understand that I was going to let them all down. I wasn't a warrior, I wasn't brave. I was just scared. I still felt like a kid, sometimes.

I shouted over the noise as loud as I could, hurting my throat, but it worked. I could hear my words over that racket. "You don't understand. You need to run. The Elden are coming for us all. Run! Fly!"

Shouts from the crowd grew louder, echoing off the castle's stone steps. Their cries went from pleading to a rumble of cheering. It was as though I'd just told them I could defeat the Elden all by myself, don't worry about a thing, it'll all be done by lunchtime. What on Earth was wrong with these people?

I looked around, trying to spot the Wolands who should have been protecting me, but I couldn't see anything but the crowd as it surged forward. Some people in the crowd held their kids up at me like they were lion cubs. I knew they would all be gone soon, parents and kids. Their faces burned into my mind, and I saw them wherever I looked, like an afterglow from a bright light.

They wouldn't listen. The Elden were coming, and I couldn't save them. I'd have to—

I felt a tingle in my mind. I grabbed at my head as I sensed the darkness grow around Ochana and press inward. After a few seconds, though, the shell of dark reached the wards that protected the floating island. For the moment, it had stopped creeping tighter around the island. When it hit the wards, the shadow-like substance shuddered like it was straining as hard as it could to break through. As it pressed harder still, the shadow grew even darker, until it blocked out almost all the sun's light, making it look like dusk.

From the corner of my eye, I spotted water droplets from Ochana's crystal-pure waterfall begin to rise up into the air. Once beautiful, the waters looked sinister and putrid as they rose higher and higher, spreading out as they went. In less than a minute, the fouled water had spread to coat the inside of the protective wards, like a bubble.

A glimmer overtook the bubble like a million little, dazzling stars. The sight on any other day would have been beautiful if it wasn't for the danger we were in. My stomach dropped as I realized what was going on. Ochana's waters had coated the magical protection keeping us all alive and now it was freezing. It looked just like Paraiso's spirit water had when it froze—Eldrick's cruel way of stealing almost all the Elven tilium. Was that what was happening here?

I didn't want to think about that right now. I had more urgent things to worry about, like staying alive. I shouted to warn the other dragons, but the crowd's roaring cheer drowned out my voice again. Couldn't they see the danger we were in? I thought it must have been Eldrick using some magical trick. Then I tried to run, but no matter how hard I pumped my legs, I wasn't going anywhere. I was stuck there, forced to watch and be a part of whatever was about to happen.

The thin, frozen shell cracked. I hated to be reminded of the tragic things that happened at Paraiso, but the way this ice was cracking was a terrifying replay of what had happened there, even down to the exact sounds the ice had made. It was like a recording. Every crack and tinkle noise was the same as it had been the first time in the elven homeland.

Suddenly, the ice shattered. Frozen shards rained down on us like broken glass. Dragons in the crowd cried out when the razor-sharp ice shards hit them.

I pushed my mahier senses outward as I tried to find Eldrick, but I felt something missing. For a second, I thought back to the first time I'd gone camping with my parents, and I had woken up in the middle of the night scared for some reason. It had taken me a minute to realize that everything seemed wrong that night because there was no city noise. Something I'd never realized was there had been missing, and I had felt it before figuring out why I felt it.

This was like that. What was missing, though?

The wards! I could *feel* the wards missing. I quickly looked up, expecting to see something terrible happening because the wards were gone. The darkness, which had been straining against the wards, jerked into motion when the resistance vanished, bearing down on Ochana again, along with me and all the dragons, but it was now going even faster. There was a vibration in the air as it snapped forward.

I screamed, but no sound came out. My lungs felt like they were full of water, like the air had turned into gelatin inside me, and it hurt deep inside my chest. I panicked, but still couldn't do anything more than run in place.

The approaching darkness seemed to form a face. A terrible, huge, menacing face. Glowing orange eyes were like spotlights that only lit up one person—me. The Dragon Prince shouldn't have been so terrified that he screamed, but that's what I did. Or I tried to, but failed because I still felt like I had breathed in a lungful of jelly. My mind reeled, and I couldn't think of anything to do but stand there, screaming in silence and trying to warn everyone.

Even with so many of them downed by shards of ice, my people still looked at me with hope shining in their eyes. It was like they couldn't see the icy doom all around them, or Eldrick's laughing, snarling face. Why didn't they move out of the way? My eyes grew teary. I failed them, but could it ever have ended another way? I'd been trying to tell everyone I was going to fail them ever since I'd come to Ochana, and now it had come true.

Just before the darkness reached the crowd, I felt the energy inside me spin, making my vision whirl. Silver sparks came from my fingertips, like sparklers on the Fourth of July. I had felt that before. My tilium was almost at capacity—and there was nothing I could do about it, not with the whole crowd standing in front of me. If I just let it go and overflow, people might be hurt.

Energy rushed through me, filling me up until I felt it pressing on my heart. As the heat inside me went from just warm to an almost painful hot, I started pouring sweat. I fought to hold it in.

My tilium grew stronger than me and burst out, shooting like spotlights from my fingers, my eyes, my mouth, until even my skin glowed and shot beams of light everywhere.

The tilium inside me flashed outward like a shockwave, washing over the crowd and my parents. I'd lost all control over it.

Where the shockwave hit the crowd, people instantly froze like glass and then shattered into thousands of pieces. It wasn't possible! That was nothing like what I had seen before, when my unstable tilium grew too big for me to hold it back.

The powerful wave kept speeding outward until it crashed into the blackness coming for us all. For a moment, I thought it might push King Eldrick's darkness away and bring the light back to Ochana. But as my tilium crashed into the darkness, it rippled and then just...vanished. My heart sank. I thought again of the ripple in a pond after throwing a pebble in, violent at first and then fading away to nothing.

The menacing face in the darkness laughed, so loud that it made my ears ring. What seemed like a black curtain crept forward, coming closer, until it closed in over us all. Eldrick's open, laughing mouth surrounded me. Everything went pitch-black.

* * *

A few moments later, light appeared in front of me. It ran like a slit from left to right and, as it widened even more, I saw huge teeth. They were easily as tall as me. The beginnings of panic stirred inside as I realized I was somehow *inside* the giant King Eldrick's mouth. Or I had shrunk, I couldn't be sure which. Nothing made sense.

I scrambled over the huge teeth, hoping to drop down to the ground below, but when I got over them, I found I was standing on something soft. I looked down to see that I was on Eldrick's bottom lip, hundreds of feet in the air. There was no way Eldrick was that tall, even as huge as he was. I was trapped in the mouth of a giant, flying Elden king.

Far below, the ground sped by, going faster and faster until the smaller details were just a blur. Far ahead, I saw something moving. Small spots dotted the ground like ants. It had to be a trick of my imagination.

A solid line reached across the grass and rocks ahead, green on one side and white on the other. I squinted to get a better look and realized there was a thick, even layer of snow. Everything was covered in ice and frost. Even the trees were white, and some were bent over from the weight of the deep snow piled on them.

The tiny dots grew larger the closer we got. I took a deep breath and willed my senses to expand, reaching out to them. I felt nothing, sensed no one. It was impossible, because I could clearly see them. My jaw dropped and my scalp tingled with shock. Far below, the missing Elves and their Troll companions laid in fear.

Each Elf and Troll was staked out, spread eagle on the ground. Over them stood Elden, some carrying whips and others with some sort of staff. Cries of pain and fear faintly carried to me on the wind. My dizziness grew, and I had to grab onto the teeth to keep from falling. I was helpless to do anything as the Elden hurt my allies, beings who had sworn to defend me with their lives. I reached out toward them, willing my mahier to bring my dragon, but nothing happened.

A deep, booming thunder washed over me, and I realized King Eldrick was laughing. It was a terrifying, evil sound.

How dare he? How could anyone do such a thing? And the Elden and Elves were cousins. My knees shook with fear, and I had to struggle to calm myself, but then I surprised myself by screaming, "You monster! Release them, now." Where had that rage suddenly come from?

The laughter grew louder, and it beat away whatever courage I had. It echoed in my head, seeming to bounce around inside my skull, driving out my thoughts. I was even more terrified.

I contemplated my fate if I jumped. Anything to get away from the terrible king. As I got ready to jump, though, I noticed that all of the Elves and Trolls had blurry faces, like pencil marks smudged with an eraser.

One single face stuck out, his smudged lines wiggling and growing together, becoming clearer until taking on the shape of Prince Gaber. He was in Paraiso. How did he get here? He had blood on his face and his eyes were wide with terror. One of the biggest, most frightening Elden I had ever seen stood over him holding a whip, which he was using with enthusiasm.

Gaber's eyes seemed to find mine and they stretched even wider in surprise. He opened his mouth, and in my mind, I could hear him pleading for me to help his Elves. Not him, but his Elves. Tears fell from my eyes. Here I was, the Keeper of Dragons, but helpless to protect the True beings as everyone said I was fated to do.

Some destiny...

Large birds that looked like buzzards flew over the vast field of Elves and Trolls. They were deep purple in color, and I wondered why I had never seen them before. And where on Earth were there purple snow buzzards? The entire scene confused me.

My attention shifted to the Elden standing over Prince Gaber. I wiped the tears from my eyes so I could see better. Something was different. Then I saw what was wrong. The Elden's massive whip was squirming. It turned and shifted like a snake. When it stopped moving, it became a thick stick, ten feet long, and at the end where the whip popper had been, now there was just one huge blade that gleamed in the bright light reflecting from the thick snow.

He laughed at Gaber, a deep, ominous cackle. The sound made my stomach drop and my eyes grow wide. He raised the new weapon over his head with both hands, ready to bring it down on Gaber. I reached out, desperate to do something, anything, but my mahier escaped me, leaving me immobilized.

My anger rose again. I was the Keeper of Dragons. Even without Eva, the Golden Dragon, I had a duty. Not only was Gaber the prince of the Elves, allies of my dragon people, but he was also my friend. Or, the closest thing I'd had to it, other than Eva.

I felt heat in my belly, growing and growing. The rage started to become painful from the heat. I realized immediately what it was—my tilium was about to overflow, *again.*

I snarled and willed my mahier to rise with my anger. Suddenly, I felt it growing inside me, building alongside the tilium. In a moment, it would be beyond my control, too.

For once the feeling of uncontrolled power didn't scare me. Instead, I focused on him; I imagined my two energies exploding from me together in a single instant, and concentrated on making it shoot down at the Elden below.

We kept streaking through the air, aiming at the huge field with all the Elves and Trolls. A thought flashed through my mind—I shouldn't be able to see Gaber in such detail from so far away. Now wasn't the time for doubt, so I shoved the thought aside.

I shouted a warrior's cry as my tilium and mahier reached the point of overflowing at the same time. I imagined my energy washing over the Elden, tearing him down to just his atoms, and—

—the giant Eldrick spit me out. "Pthooey!"

I shot through the air, spinning out of control, and I saw glimpses of his face floating above me, laughing.

The booming voice inside my skull said, "You tasted better before you cleansed it, little stealer of tilium. It's okay, though, because I have *plenty* of my own."

As I kept spinning and falling, the icy, snowy ground came up to meet me. At my speed and distance, I wouldn't survive. I tried once again to call for my dragon. With desperation giving me strength and focusing my thoughts, I called out for it, but I still didn't sense it. Where was my dragon in all this?

Why had it abandoned me now, when I needed it most? The dragon was me, I was the dragon. I still had my mahier. It should have worked.

The ground was fast approaching. The panic in the back of my mind exploded into complete terror, and I screamed in my mind, desperate for my dragon. I willed myself to shift.

My mahier flowed from me, searching and seeking. It had a mind of its own as it looked for my dragon. In another instant, I felt...something. It had grabbed onto the shockwave of my mahier, which was reaching out to find my dragon still. I saw a blinding flash, so bright that I had to shield my face. When I opened my eyes, I realized that I wasn't falling—I was flying!

I looked over and saw my wings stretched out. It was glorious. My heart soared, and my fear fled. No wonder I hadn't been able to call my dragon. I'd been the dragon the entire time. That didn't make any sense at all, though. I remembered being just plain Cole a moment before. Or had I just been too frightened to notice that I'd been the dragon that entire time? It was confusing.

I tilted to my left, and swept toward the Elves and Trolls. The ice-covered fields of snow were still several miles away. The only thing that wasn't pure white was a small mass of black spots, which had to be the Elves and Trolls. As I leveled out to head toward them, I remembered the brilliant flash of light. Had that been when I shifted?

Far above, the sky's usual blue hue suddenly seemed to split apart like sunlight hitting a crystal, and then the raw beauty of what I saw in the skies took my breath away. As far as my dragon eyes could see, in every direction, there was a multitude of colors that seemed to twist and boil across the sky, gleaming and then fading, then shining again, never the same colors twice in a row. I realized they must be the Northern Lights, though I had never seen them before. Nothing else could be so strikingly beautiful.

I shook my head hard to clear my mind of the distraction, and reluctantly turned my eyes to the scene below. I had almost reached Prince Gaber and the Elden, but King Eldrick seemed to be missing. I had the strange idea that the Northern Lights display pushed the evil king away, but with him gone, I wasn't quite as afraid as I had been.

I dove at the Elden who stood laughing over Gaber and opened my mouth, releasing a geyser of purple fire far larger than any fire-breath I'd seen among the Wolands.

Then I realized I wasn't breathing fire, but a deadly frost as cold as space. It only moved like flames. As I dove at my target, mouth still open and breathing the ice-fire, I let out all my fear and anger with one mighty roar that shook the ground...

* * *

I sat bolt upright and threw my blanket off, my scream echoing off the cabin walls before fading away. I was covered in sweat, gasping for air. My entire body felt as sore as if I had been laboring all day. I was so confused. Had the Northern Lights sent me back to Ochana? That strange, beautiful light...

No. As the sleep faded and my senses returned, I realized that I wasn't in Ochana—I was still in Paraiso. It had been a dream. I felt it slipping away, escaping my memory like most dreams do. I struggled to remember as many details as I could, but by the time my nightmare-sweat evaporated, I could only remember a single detail. It was burned into my mind, and I knew I would never forget those beautiful and frightening Northern Lights, pulsing high above a frozen land.

I climbed out of bed and picked my blanket off the floor, tossing it back to where it belonged. Nearby, I found my clothes and newly-issued sword neatly arranged.

The memory of what had happened just a handful of days before came crashing back to me. Eldrick had frozen the sacred waters of Paraiso, and with it, the Elves' tilium, leaving both Elves and Trolls powerless. They couldn't fight back when his Elden had swarmed over them and then vanished, taking the defenseless Elves and Trolls with them as prisoners.

He had also used the Farro like pawns, getting them to kidnap Eva to draw me to his swampy home in Venezuela. It got me out of Paraiso, along with the fearsome dragons and most of the warrior Elves. It let him attack their home while it was defenseless.

I smiled briefly at the memory of destroying the Farros and their ruler, Queen Tana. Their own greed and hunger for power was really what destroyed them. The first time they had attacked the dragons, I tore their dark tilium from them with Eva's help and drew it into myself, but nothing that foul could *stay* evil inside the Keeper of Dragons. Somehow, I had cleansed it and turned it pure. When Queen Tana and her Farros ripped their tilium back from me, they drew it into themselves greedily. Dark souls and purified tilium were a bad combination, and it had cost them all their lives.

I let out a deep breath, sat on the bed, and let the nightmare's tension drain away. I knew what that dream had been about. Basically, my own insecurities. But the land of ice and snow with the Northern Lights, there at the end...it certainly hadn't felt like a dream. Deep inside, I was convinced there was something important about it. But if it was a message, who had sent it?

I didn't know what it all meant, but I had to tell Jericho, no matter what sort of training or missions they had all decided to put on me for the day. Those could wait. This was more important.

Jericho's deep voice boomed in my head, startling me. "Cole, you're sleeping the day away while a war rages. I'm at the command center. Come find me immediately."

Jericho sounded more irritated than usual, but I thought I heard an edge of fear in his voice. Usually he was just angry or grumpy, so it had me a bit worried. I wanted to talk to him about my dream anyway, so I jumped out of bed and headed down from my borrowed treehouse.

Chapter Two

My feet thudded across the twisting sky-bridges of Paraiso. There didn't seem to be any pattern, but I had a sense there was one. I just hadn't been there long enough to see it. I had only recently remembered how to get from my assigned cabin to Gaber's command center. It was lucky I did, because Eva wasn't around. She knew the paths better than I did, so I usually just followed her. I was on my own this day, though.

When I got to a place I thought was near the command center, I let my mahier reach out, trying to sense Jericho. He was down there, and I grinned for a moment, happy to have gotten it right this time. Deciding to jump down, I let my dragon take me on wings to the jungle floor, rather than zapping there or climbing down. I really did need to figure out how I zapped last time. My first night here in Paraiso felt like forever ago.

Once I reached the ground, I called to my human, then walked to the command center. The first person I saw was Jericho, the leader of the Wolands—the red dragon warriors who defended all dragons. His eyes were glowing bright red as he talked to Gaber and Cairo. Few people were brave enough to stand up to Jericho when he was angry, but the Elven Prince Gaber looked as smug as ever, even with the dimness in his eyes. I couldn't imagine the turmoil he must be feeling. Almost all of his Elves and Troll allies had been kidnapped, his sister included. I shook the thought away as I continued my assessment of the room.

Cairo was standing his ground for once, too. He was another red dragon, and his job was to protect Eva. He thought they were soulmates, *Verum Salit*, though he had yet to inform Eva of this.

King Evander of the Trolls was there, too, but he stood back a bit, talking to an Elf soldier I recognized as Bran. He, too, had lost so much. It was evident by his ragged appearance he was failing at staying strong. Evander's green hair stuck up everywhere and the bags under his eyes did nothing to hide his lack of sleep.

With Cairo there, I looked around the room for Eva. Sure enough, I spotted her sitting alone in a chair off to one side. She was my best friend as a human, and now she was the Golden Dragon, half of the Keeper of Dragons. For some reason, everyone seemed to think that she and I would save the day together. I had doubts about that. I nodded to her and she rewarded me with a sad smile.

Jericho looked almost agitated enough to begin billowing smoke. Cairo finally looked away, even though he was one of Ochana's best warriors. Gaber didn't. I had no idea what had Jericho riled up. Not that he wasn't always wound tight, but today he seemed ready to blow.

I gave Gaber and Evander a slight bow after I stepped through the door. Jericho looked from Cairo to me, and everyone else went silent, too, and turned to watch. I wished I knew what was going on, but Jericho hadn't told me. I gathered up my courage and said, "Morning, I came as quickly as I could."

He rolled his eyes. "What else would you do, sit in your room? We don't have time for idle chatter. We need to talk about what to do for the missing Trolls and Elves. They're our allies, and we let them down once while we hid with our heads in the sand."

Gaber snorted and said, "To your everlasting shame."

Jericho kept his eyes on me, ignoring Gaber. "We will not let them down again," he said, and drove his fist into his palm.

Cairo bowed to me, like most of the dragons did, then said to Jericho, "Eva has the right idea."

Gaber coughed, catching our attention. His smirk was contagious. I guess it amused him that everyone turned to him. I could almost hear him thinking, *made you look!* He said, "I like Eva. For a Dramon, she's pretty nice. But I'm not sure her idea holds water."

Cairo said, "She did make it sound pretty convincing. We travel to the Mermaids and ask for their help. We need to bring them into the Elven Alliance, anyway."

I knew very little about the Mermaids. I knew they had their own form of magic, very similar to tilium, and that they didn't interact with others often. Other than that, they were a mystery to me. Just another creature I thought didn't exist, much like dragons.

Jericho's eyes flared a brighter red. "That's foolish. We need to find the other Fairies in Greece and see if they'll join us. We can get extra help that way, and we owe Queen Annabelle and her Fairies at least that much, don't you think? They fought bravely by our side, and they, too, have lost some of their own. Besides, Fairy tilium is strong, and the Mermaids can't do much for us in this war. If the Elden lived at the bottom of the sea, you'd have a point."

Gaber leaped to his feet. "At least I can believe that from a dragon. Leave it to them to ignore a whole race because it's not useful at the moment. It isn't the first time."

My single strongest memory from the nightmare came back to me, then. Before Jericho could bicker some more with Gaber, I decided to argue the point about the Mermaids. From the corner of my eye, though, I caught Eva shaking her head at me. She raised her eyebrows and her eyes were as wide as she could make them go. She was giving me a warning to stay quiet, thanks to reading my mind again. But why should I be quiet? I was going to have to tell Jericho soon, either way.

Cairo looked angry, but bowed his head in submission. I thought he looked tense and stiff-necked when he did it, though, and I worried that he might be about to take a swing at Jericho, or at Gaber. Probably Jericho. He said, "Compared to the Elden, there are only a few Fairies in Greece. And besides—"

Jericho cut him off with a bark. "Numbers aren't the question, and you know it. No one is more motivated to help Elves and Trolls than Fairies, even if they have to team up with a dragon to do it. And the Fairies also suffered while we dragons were thinking about other things. We owe Fairies just as much as we owe the Elves. If we don't bring the Greek Fairies into this, would Queen Annabelle ever forgive us? We need her as an ally in spirit, not just a formality."

I could see how irritated Eva was as she snapped, "But what about everything I heard about the mereum? They say it has the ability to—"

Jericho growled, interrupting her. He was good at interrupting people. "No. They never allow outsiders to try it. Only Mermaids have ever traveled that maze, not since the first Elf walked through the reef and created it in the first place. The maze's powers are strong, sure, and its tilium might even be a match for the Elden, but it's all useless to us out there in the ocean."

Gaber rolled his eyes, but I watched Eva, not him. She squinted at Jericho. She was brave and reckless, and she looked ready to say something she would regret.

She had already warned me not to do the same thing, and she'd been right, so I jumped into the conversation before she could reply. "We should listen to Eva, and if not her, then to Cairo. They both think the Mermaids are the best idea. I don't know anything about them, but..." My voice trailed off as I tried to think of what to say next. I knew I'd just lost any chance at convincing Jericho.

He laughed, little smoke rings coming from his nose. "It seems you're right—you don't know what you're talking about. Eva can speak for herself, but why are we even discussing Mermaids? Stick to what you know, Cole, that's lesson number four."

I felt my anger rising. Just because he was the high and mighty Jericho, he didn't have the right to ignore people or talk to them that way, especially when the other people might be right. And *definitely* not if those people were the Keeper of Dragons.

He turned his attention back to Cairo, not even waiting for me to reply. He shouted, "*Your* duty is the protection of the Golden Dragon. *My* duty is the protection of Ochana and all that is True. Do your own job, and let me do mine. We need to go to Greece and rally the other Fairies. It's our only real choice. Fairies have the strongest power in the world, other than dragon mahier, and we can't even get to the Mermaids fast enough to make a difference in this war. You know they move around all the time."

I listened and clenched my jaw. Even Jericho could be wrong.

But my dream kept pressing at me, and I decided it couldn't wait any longer, despite Eva's warning. I raised my voice above the noise and said, "Actually, there's a third option." I hoped I sounded steady and confident.

Everyone turned to me again, but I forced myself to stand tall. I looked each of them right in the eyes. My nightmare clues were important. "I had a nightmare last night, and part of it was more than just a dream. It was a *message.*"

"A message?" Jericho eyed me warily.

"I had a vision of the Elden somewhere in a land of snow and ice. They were torturing the missing Elves and Trolls. There were lights in the sky, beautiful lights. The Aurora Borealis, I think. We need to find our missing friends while we still have time to save them. To do that, we need to look in a place like the one I saw. North, not east to Greece or the Dead Sea."

Jericho let out three odd sounds, hollow and deep, from the back of his throat. I realized he was actually laughing. I wasn't sure I'd ever heard him laugh before. "Colton, I know you think you have some sort of a clue, but it was only a dream. None of your training has been in dream interpretation. But even if you had the training, could you trust it with the way your training has gone so far? The only area you are even close to keeping up with is your sword. What makes you think you know what that dream meant?"

I gritted my teeth in frustration. If I was fated to save the world from the Time of Fear, he should be listening, not barking orders. It had been more than some random nightmare. I *knew* it, deep in my gut. "It wasn't just a dream, it was—"

He cut me off again, saying, "No. We're not going to abandon our duties and go pursue a dream. Not even a dream, but a silly nightmare. After we get to the Greek Fairies, then we can send Realm Two to explore the far north, just to make you feel better, but I won't waste precious resources on it. We're at war, my prince, and half of winning it will be to manage our resources well. The rest of us have to deal with the real world, and you might want to join us there."

"It's not abandoning our duties," I said. I was desperate to make them believe me. Too much depended on this. "I'm telling you, it was a clue or a warning. I don't know which. But I do know it was important, and we should go look."

As Jericho's eyes flared red again, little puffs of smoke came from his nostrils. He wasn't used to anyone challenging him, especially me, and he sure wasn't laughing anymore.

Eva stepped between the two of us, facing me. "We all know dreams are just our subconscious fears getting worked out." She paused for a moment, hands on her hips as she cocked her head to the side. I had the feeling she was sizing me up, and it felt awkward.

She said, "What else was in this dream besides snow, lights in the sky, and our missing allies?"

My mind raced as I tried to figure out how to explain everything. I wished I remembered more of my nightmare. The purple buzzards must have been simple dream stuff, but the rest was *real*. It definitely felt real. Eldrick swallowed Ochana, then whisked me away to somewhere up north. That's where we would find the Elves and Trolls, and Ochana was in danger. I had to get them to understand.

Eva laughed out loud, and I lost my train of thought. When she saw the irritation on my face, she touched my shoulder. "I'm sorry, Cole. I don't mean to laugh. But purple buzzards? A giant King Eldrick flying around? Come on, it's normal nightmare stuff. I get that it bothered you, but that doesn't mean it was important. Dreams just let you know what you're afraid of. Instead of focusing on your fears and a dream, we need to focus on something real, right?"

It didn't usually bug me when she read my thoughts, because it made me feel like we were somehow closer. Together we were the Keeper of Dragons, and best friends. But this time, it felt like she had invaded my privacy. "I know the difference between a regular dream and a warning."

She shook her head, eyes showing sympathy for me. I knew she could feel my conflicted emotions radiating from me. "I'm sorry. I'm not ignoring how you feel, but you might be still feeling the nightmare's effects. You need to let that go, Cole. Dreams can't hurt you, no matter how real they feel."

She turned around to face Jericho, who had been standing there smirking at me. She started in on Jericho again about how we should go to the Mermaids. Her whole argument boiled down to the fact that Earth was mostly water, and that was the domain of Mermaids. They were like hermits, I had heard, so outsiders usually didn't know much about them.

Jericho snapped, "Yes, but Elden aren't water-breathers. The Greek Fairies are the ones who can help us deal with Eldrick up here on dry land, where the Elves and Trolls are. What don't you get about this?"

I turned away from their arguing and wandered over to a chair, sitting with a thump. When they ignored me, it bothered me. More than it should have. I knew my dream sounded weird, and taking a stupid dream so seriously was also weird, but one of them should care how I felt about it.

The dragons pulled me out of their toolbox when they needed something from me, but the rest of the time, they wanted me in that box where I wouldn't be in their way.

There was a sharp noise, and I looked over to see Jericho clapping his hands. He said, "No more of this. I'll discuss it with the Council, but for now, it's time for the Keeper of Dragons' training." He turned to look directly at me and said, "Your first session for today is in the arena. We need to get you more comfortable with your sword. Meet me over in the clearing by the shore in five minutes."

Then he turned away to talk to Cairo again. They had put me in the toolbox yet again. I let out a frustrated sigh and headed toward the lakeshore. More arena training... Well, that was fine with me. I was kind of angry, and I felt ready to let off some steam.

On my first step, my stomach began to churn, and I stopped in my tracks. I felt suddenly hot and started to sweat. I shook my head to clear the feeling and took another step, but then my vision began to spin, faster and faster. When my stomach cramped up, pain shot through me like a lightning bolt. Everything looked like it slid downward—my eyes rolling back?—leaving only darkness.

I felt myself falling over backward. It all went pitch black for a second, but then I saw a blinding light ahead. I squinted, then gasped. Far below me was a flat field, covered in snow and ice.

J.A. Culican

Chapter Three

I struggled against the darkness and clawed my way back toward the light, then slowly peeled my aching eyes open. Eva and Jericho stood over me, one on either side, looking concerned. The vision I'd seen was still fresh in my memory as my fuzzy mind cleared.

Eva said, "Are you okay? What happened?" She chewed lightly on her bottom lip, her nervous habit.

I nodded and propped myself up on my elbows. "I'm fine. Just a little dizzy. I didn't get a chance to grab breakfast."

That wasn't the entire truth. In my vision, I went back to the land of ice and snow and saw a scene a lot like the last time. King Eldrick wasn't there, but within the crowd of Elves and Trolls tied up, I saw Mel and Clara looking up at me. Somehow, I could see their faces close up, even though the crowd had been far away. They both spoke together, warning me, "Be careful. They have a trap waiting."

I'd only had a glimpse, but it had that same weird, real feeling as the nightmare. I was sure it wasn't just a vision—it was a message. I couldn't have explained how I knew that, but there was no point in bringing it up anyway. They would just push it aside and ignore me again. But I knew the truth.

Jericho rolled his eyes, throwing an apple at me. "If you're fine, and you're done messing around, we have work to do. Into the arena, both of you."

I was a little angry that he didn't give me some time off after my vision hit, but he had a sense of urgency I hadn't heard from him before. It was like he was afraid, which kind of scared me a little. Jericho was never afraid.

Over the next hour, Eva and I trained hard. I showed a little bit of improvement, but my performance was still embarrassing. Every time I connected with a jab or hit my opponent with a leg sweep, they turned around and knocked me into the dirt.

That was frustrating, but I was more concerned about Eva than about how I was doing. Every time I glanced at her, she seemed to be moving in slow motion. Her heart just wasn't in it, like she didn't have any motivation, and she kept getting knocked down.

That was surprising because before that, she had been advancing quickly. Now, even I was doing better than her, and it hadn't gone unnoticed. Every few seconds, Jericho barked at her. Normally, she had a quick reply and a sharp, witty answer, but today she was suffering his insults in silence. She hadn't even been looking him in the eyes, and gave only short replies. I thought she spent a lot of time looking at the ground. That was definitely not how my best friend usually acted. I was a bit worried.

When the shout went out to break up the matches, I made sure I was in line for water next to her. She gave me a faint, forced smile. I really wanted to give her some encouragement, because she looked way down in the dumps.

Once we got our water, she walked to an empty corner in the little arena field, and I followed. When she sat on a stool to rest, I pulled one over and sat with her. After a long drink from my canteen, I said, "Hey. You feeling okay?" I gave her what I hoped was a reassuring smile.

She took a short drink of water and then rested her arms on her knees as she bent forward, looking down at the ground. She didn't answer for a few seconds, but just when I thought she might ignore me completely, she looked up and said, "I'm frustrated, Cole. I don't know why I'm struggling with the training. I was doing so great before, but now I just feel... I don't know. Weak, I guess."

That came as a real shock. She was always confident, and seeing her like this was kind of depressing. I needed to cheer my best friend up. "Yeah, I saw you out there. I thought maybe you were feeling sick, but I'm surprised to hear you talk like this. I mean, you flew through the training floors in Ochana way faster than me. I haven't even really advanced yet, but you went up a floor in the first week, right?"

She just shook her head, and her eyes grew red-rimmed. If she started crying, I had no idea what I would do. Should I put my arm around her? Try to comfort her, somehow? I just didn't know. This was Eva, after all, and she was always stronger than me.

She said, "You're wrong, Cole. All these things we're doing to save Ochana... It's not *me* finding a way through them, it's *you*. It doesn't matter how my training was going, because it's not going well right now. That's just like when we were dealing with the Farro and the Elden. All I did was get lost and get knocked out. You had to rescue me, and it almost cost us everything. I'm totally doubting my whole right to be the Golden Dragon."

I was stunned, but I knew she was wrong. She was sharing the same thoughts I'd had since coming to Ochana, and it hurt to see that. I said, "I haven't really done anything. It might've happened *through* me, but I was just along for the ride."

"I just feel useless. I miss home and all my friends. I came here because it seemed like the right thing to do, and because I didn't want to put my parents in danger. And you needed me, and we're friends, you know? But I have to wonder if I did the right thing. Maybe you're better off without me."

I took a chance and put my arm around her shoulder, and we just sat in silence for a minute. She was always there for me when I felt down, so being there for her was the least I could do. Besides, she deserved it, and she was being too hard on herself. "I can't really believe you feel this way. I mean, whatever I did to the Farro, I couldn't have done it without you. Together, we're a team. We're the Keeper of Dragons. I know it's rough right now, but in the end, it's not going to be me who saves us all. It's going to be you and me together. There are lots of people counting on us, good people who deserve help. Even if we fail, we have to try, right? When I get doubts, I ask myself, 'What would Eva do?' So you can't be like this or I'm going to be really confused next time."

She didn't laugh. She just kept silent. I didn't know what else to say, so I squeezed her tighter for a second. Maybe a little gesture could help her see how strong she was. Definitely stronger than me, not to mention braver. She had a confidence I never did, and sometimes that was the only thing keeping me going. I couldn't afford to lose that now, so I just sat with her until the shout went out to train again.

I stood and held my hand out toward her, offering to help her up, but she batted my hand aside and popped up to her feet. She looked me in the eyes for a couple seconds, and there was a fierce look in them. Was she back to normal, or did I upset her?

She walked away with her head down and her fists closed, but she didn't head back to the field. She was walking into the jungle. Where was she going? I looked for Jericho but didn't see him. I saw Cairo, though, already jogging after her. He was only a dozen steps behind her when she reached the tree line.

I shook my head. Nothing I said seemed to help. I let out a frustrated sigh and went back to my training.

Half an hour later, Jericho shouted for the day's training to end, and not a minute too soon. I was totally exhausted. My whole body ached from the training. I would be surprised if I didn't have a dozen huge bruises tomorrow morning. My legs felt weak and rubbery from all the effort.

Cairo and Eva still weren't back, so I returned to my treetop room. Inside, I looked around for any clue that someone had been in there, but didn't see anything. I checked the places someone could have hidden—Jericho's advice to always be alert and never trust anyone made sense with everything that had happened recently. We were in a warzone, and it made sense to be careful.

I glanced at my bed as if it had called out to me: "Sleep! Come and sleep on me." That sounded like a great idea. I could get a nap and maybe feel a little better before my next training. It would probably be training with Gaber, so I needed to get control of my tilium. I took off my boots and my jacket, got into bed, and stared up at the ceiling. In moments, I felt myself drifting off into a warm, fuzzy, and very welcome sleep.

The shrill and sudden sound of someone screaming made me bolt upright in bed. Only half-awake, I listened carefully. Were we being attacked, or had I been dreaming?

Another scream echoed around me, and I recognized the voice. It was Eva. A chill ran up my spine as I leaped out of bed, grabbed my sword and ran for the door.

J.A. Culican

Chapter Four

When I was halfway across the first tree bridge, I used my tilium and blinked down to the jungle floor. I didn't have time to wander around up there because from the sound of Eva's voice, she was on the ground somewhere. I didn't know the paths well enough yet to find my way.

Once on the ground, I wondered where my guardians were, but I had no time to go look for them. I put my head down as I sprinted toward where I thought her scream came from. As I ran, she screamed again. This time, she sounded closer, like she was directly in front of me, but so was the maze of jungle. I had wandered the jungle enough since I got here to know how to find my way through. I was learning what to look for to find the clearer paths.

Seconds later, I emerged into a large clearing and skidded to a halt. My eyes bugged wide as I took in the scene. Eva was sprinting toward me from the other side, and right on her heels were four huge Carnites. They were practically giants; I'd seen them rip up trees by their roots. Well, I had heard them do it and seen the damage later.

Without hesitating, by reflex, I reached out with my mahier and summoned my dragon. The transformation happened almost instantly, and I barreled toward her.

Far away, other creatures began to scream. The Carnites must have invaded the entire area, but I was here and so was Eva. I couldn't help them, but I could help her. Together, I thought we might be strong enough to survive this.

In moments, I had reached the first Carnite. At the last second, I tipped my wings and streaked upward with my claws in front of me, raking the monster. My claws dug into its thick hide, and it crashed to the ground. I wished I had control of my fire, for this would be the perfect time to use it. Jericho would tell me to conserve my mahier and fire would definitely diminish it, but I had a feeling it would help us with this fight. I spun around and flew back. When I swooped past Eva, running the other direction, I landed by her and turned back into my human.

Her eyes were wide, full of fear, but she stopped when I landed by her. We both drew swords; the other three Carnites would be on us in seconds, and the one I'd knocked over was scrambling to its feet. It wasn't bleeding, though, and I realized my claws had only torn up bits of its thick hide without really hurting it.

How on Earth could we defeat these monsters? The whole area could be full of Carnites by now, for all I knew. "There's nowhere to run, Eva. We take out the one in front first." That's all I had time to say before the Carnite reached us. It carried a huge club, an uprooted tree, and it swung down at us. We charged to meet it.

Running at top speed, with my full momentum behind me, I dove through the air and somersaulted when I landed, so I ended up back on my feet and running. Eva did the same. A moment later, I leaped into the air as I passed the monster, swinging my sword at its belly as I flew by. Thank goodness we had been training with our swords daily since the

Elves and Trolls were kidnapped. It still felt awkward at times in my hand, but at this very moment, I felt invincible.

Eva spun and swung her sword at its ankle as she passed, and finished her spin so that she ended up facing the same direction she had been traveling. We both kept running, leaving the Carnite behind us. I didn't know if we'd hurt it, though.

With two Carnites knocked over behind us and two on their feet up ahead, I knew we were in trouble. We had let them surround us. I felt panic rising up, and I struggled to keep it under control. I had to be able to think clearly.

"On the left," I cried out as we ran. Then we would only have to deal with one Carnite between us and escape. Still, that one could do a lot of damage.

As we approached the one on the left, it swept its tree trunk club at us over the ground, left to right, instead of swinging it overhead like the last one. As the club came at me, I jumped and used my mahier to carry me over the deadly weapon. I had no idea how I did it, but it worked. I passed right over the club as my mahier turned my jump into a leap.

When I hit the ground, though, my ankle turned. Not enough to injure me, but I fell in a heap.

I glanced around for Eva, but couldn't see her. She must have run into the jungle. I jumped to my feet, but had gotten up too late. One Carnite was swinging its club right at me, and I grit my teeth, bracing for a hit that would probably kill me. It came at me faster than I thought possible as it moved in an arc over me and then came streaking down. My last thought was to hope that Eva had escaped.

When it was just a couple feet from my head, though, it froze in midair. Confused, I stared at the club that hung above me. Two lines of bright light were wrapped around the club on one end, and stretched behind me.

I risked a glance back and saw two Wolands a few feet away, standing with their hands outstretched. They must have used their mahier to bind the club, I realized. I scrambled away from the Carnite in a panic.

The creature roared. It shifted its weight and swung its club to the side, and the two guards flew through the air, mahier still bound to it. One landed in the dirt and rolled, but the other struck a tree. I heard a loud snap and hoped it was just a branch breaking. He bounced off and hit the ground, then lay still.

The other scrambled to his feet in an instant, but he wasn't fast enough. Another Carnite leaped through the air, swinging its club over its head. When it hit the guardian, it buried itself halfway into the soft jungle floor.

With a shout, I jumped at the Carnite in front of me, landing at its feet. It was raising its club, so I used my momentum to somersault between its legs, swinging my sword with all my might as I rolled by. I came up on my feet with our backs facing each other, and I heard a pain-filled roar behind me. I grinned.

Then, to my left, Eva ran out of the jungle. "We have to fall back, Cole." Her eyes were wide, and if the fearless Eva looked scared, I definitely took her word for it. I turned to run back into the jungle with her.

I suddenly found myself flying through the air end over end, spinning fast enough that the sky and the ground flickered into view, one after the other. I felt pain throughout my body, and I caught a glimpse of Eva beside me, looking like a limp rag doll as she spun. I spotted the Carnite I had just cut, one foot in the air in front of it, and realized it had punted us like footballs. We landed in the soft dirt together, tumbling and flopping as we came to a stop.

I tried to get up, but my body wasn't responding. All the fight had been knocked out of me. The Carnite wasted no time, running toward us with its club held over its head in both hands. As that club came down toward me for a second time, all I could do was roll and scramble away from it on my hands and knees, trying to get to my feet but stumbling.

It walked into striking distance again and roared like an animal in rage and pain, and I understood how it felt. I was sure I'd have internal injuries from being kicked, and there was no way I would survive a hit from that club. As if in slow motion, the club began its decent toward me.

I saw a red streak, a blur of smoke and fire that flew through the air and smashed into the club, knocking it flying from the Carnite's hands. The huge red dragon that had struck it bounced off and landed in a heap. I recognized Jericho. He had saved my life.

Two more Woland guards arrived with him, shifting into their human forms and pulling their swords as they landed next to me. One reached down and grabbed me, yanking me to my feet; the other did the same to Eva. Neither of them looked at Jericho, and it occurred to me they didn't know he was here.

I pointed, and they nodded. Then they sprinted straight at the Carnite. One climbed up its back and the other swung his blade into its belly. I couldn't stab it without risk of hitting the guards, so I ran to Jericho. I reached out with my mahier as I ran, trying to see if he was injured as I opened up my senses. To Eva, running next to me, I said, "He's alive."

Jericho was stirring when we got to him, and we bent down to help him up. Smoke puffed from his nostrils as he shifted to human form. He looked bad, with most of his face already swelling, the black and blue beginning to show. I assumed the rest of his body was just as bad, maybe worse. He shouted, "We have to fall back. The Keepers must be kept safe!"

I didn't feel like arguing. We ran, Jericho staggering between us.

J.A. Culican

Chapter Five

Eva and I made a break for it, half-carrying and half-dragging Jericho. With every step, he groaned in pain, but there was nothing we could do about it out here in the jungle. Behind us, the Realm Five dragons were blocking any Carnite chasing us. I felt bad about leaving them behind, but we had to get Jericho out of there.

Eva read my mind again, I guess, because she grunted and said, "I feel bad, too, but that's their job. We defend the True, and they defend us. Now focus. We have to get out of here."

I had begun to sweat and had to pause to shift my grip on Jericho. He groaned, but then his eyes flicked open and he looked at me. "We...have to retreat...away from Paraiso."

He was right, but if an army of Carnites wandered into Paraiso with its wards down and its tilium gone, the few free Trolls and Elves that remained would be lost.

"Eva," I said between gasps for air, "we need to head away from Paraiso. Maybe we can lure the Carnites away."

She didn't answer, but we turned east to move away from the Elves' home. I looked back once, wishing we could go there. Paraiso had been a paradise that felt like home more than Ochana did, but now it was powerless and almost abandoned.

We staggered through the jungle as fast as we could. At one spot, the canopy above us opened up and I caught a glimpse of the sun. It told me we'd been running for at least an hour.

I could still hear the Carnites crashing through the jungle behind us, but we had gained some distance. "We have to stop for a minute. We need to check on Jericho. You feel him sweating? That can't be good," I said, gasping.

"He's in shock," Eva said, and I could hear concern in her voice. "Lay him down gently."

We stopped and lowered him to the jungle floor. I pulled out my water skin and knelt beside him.

"Can you hear me? You need some water. No, not too much... There we go, just sip at it."

I stood and stretched my back, looking around to check out our situation. None of the landmarks looked familiar. Then again, I didn't grow up in the jungle. I had no idea how far from Paraiso we were.

"I hoped he would come around while we ran," I said, "but he's hurt worse than I thought. We need to get him to Ochana, or I think he might die."

Jericho's eyes seemed to focus again. Faint and weak, he said, "We're about five miles from Paraiso." Then he coughed, and his whole body shook. I saw a trickle of blood from the corner of his mouth, and he grew pale. His eyes rolled up and he passed out again. I hoped he'd wake up a little before we had to continue running for our lives.

Eva put her fists on her hips and let out a sharp breath, then said, "You're right. I wanted to get farther away before we made any decisions, but I don't think Jericho can wait. We're just going to have to hope we're far enough away. What do you think?"

"I think they were just a wandering band who stumbled into Paraiso's territory, now that the wards are down. Either way, if they knew where Paraiso was, I don't think we could have drawn them away like this."

Eva gave me a curt nod. "Then it's decided. We get Jericho out of here and hope we don't accidentally draw attention to Paraiso. But there's one more problem."

I frowned. "Another problem?"

"He's too weak to hold on, much less fly. One of us is going to have to hold him."

I hadn't thought of that. She was right, it was a problem. "I don't think you're big enough to carry us both so far. I'll have to do it."

She nodded, but said, "Do you think you can? We're already tired from carrying him through this jungle."

I rolled my shoulders in circles, stretching my muscles a bit. I would need those to fly. I didn't feel any strains or other injuries, though, despite being kicked for a field goal by a Carnite earlier, and an hour-long scramble through the jungle. "I think I can at least make it to Ellesmere Island. From there, we can call in for help from Ochana."

She pursed her lips and nodded. I didn't blame her for being unhappy about the situation. If I cramped up over the Atlantic...

She motioned for me to get going and it looked like it was time for me to step up. The idea of me saving Jericho seemed somehow wrong. I didn't even have full control of my mahier, and I was a terrible warrior. But I was the only one who might be able to help him.

I swore to myself that I would never bring this up to him again, if he lived. Then I walked a few feet away and called to my dragon. Claws shot out through my fingertips and my many-colored scales rose up through my skin. My wings burst out as I stretched them wide over some of the smaller trees.

The transition was the smoothest one yet, even though I was exhausted. Quickly, I found my bearings and focused on the task at hand. I concentrated on sending my thoughts to Eva. "Can you get him on my back?"

She bent over and struggled to pick up the half-conscious Jericho. The water bottle fell from his hands, but we left it there. I had another. It took her a few minutes of grunting and sweating to get him in place, then a couple more minutes for her to get him situated and secure between her arms as she sat behind him. She said, "All right, let's see what you got, Cole."

I took a couple of steps and jumped. I beat down with my wings and rose a few feet into the air. But I didn't have enough speed and landed hard. Eva and Jericho almost fell from my back.

I felt Eva patting my side. She said, "It's okay, Cole. You can do this. Try again, but reach out with your mahier, too. Let it flow through you and help push you off the ground."

I launched myself into the air again, beating my wings hard. Summoning my power, I reached out with it just like I would if I was expanding my senses, but instead of seeing or feeling, I willed it to push me away from the ground. Energy flew through me, pushing, and I suddenly felt lighter. It worked. I had the little bit of speed I needed to have more lift. Excited, I flapped hard and we slowly rose up.

I still had my energy pushing down on the ground, and so I sensed it when the Carnites rushed into the clearing. One jumped as high as it could and swung its club, but it missed by at least ten feet. It was sort of scary to realize that if we had waited another minute, they would have caught us.

I thought of Realm Five, who had stayed behind to buy us time to escape, but I couldn't feel them. Hopefully, they were simply too far away to sense, but I worried about them. They may have given themselves up to let us escape.

The thought was too sad. I pushed it from my mind and focused on flying. Faster and faster, higher and higher over the jungle. I only hoped I could keep that up. It would take hours to get to Ellesmere Island.

* * *

With all that weight on my back, it took me half an hour to get up to a good altitude. When I got to the right height, though, flying got a lot easier. Something about wind drag and air pressure, from what little I remembered in my studies. Most of my concentration went into using my mahier to keep Eva and Jericho from being tossed off by the winds. I left it to her to keep any humans on the ground from seeing us.

About a half an hour after that, I saw the glittering, beautiful Atlantic Ocean ahead of us. We were nearing Africa's west coast. I focused on Eva and thought at her: "I'm getting tired. I need to land, stretch a bit, and rest my wings. Plus, I could literally eat a horse."

I heard her shouting, "I'm sure you're starving by now."

"Maybe hungrier than I've ever been!"

"Going back and forth between human and dragon eats up your mahier. And don't forget you've been keeping us safe back here. You need to refuel. You know what that means, right?"

To the north, farms stretched along the shore. I angled down, and we gained speed as I lost altitude, heading for the shoreline.

Eva said, "You have to land away from the farms, call your human and drop us off, and go find some horses. Or better yet, a cow."

I felt a little guilty at the thought of eating someone else's cattle, or whatever a group of horses was called, but Jericho's life and the war against the Elden were far more important. If they won the war, the humans would be in for a lot more trouble than just a missing horse or cow. I decided I'd have to do it, even if I felt bad about it.

When we got close to the ground, I put my wings back to slow us and then drifted down, landing on my hind legs. For once, I didn't do a faceplant when my front legs hit the dirt. Eva dragged Jericho off my back, trying to be gentle on him. As a dragon, I couldn't do much to help, so she grunted and struggled on her own. When he finally came free, she fell over backward and he landed on top of her. At least she broke his fall.

"Oh yeah, at least I broke his fall. Thanks, Cole." She flashed a smile, so I knew wasn't really upset. I did wish she would stop randomly hearing my thoughts, though.

I called my human, and the transformation was quick. I rolled my shoulders and stretched my arms out, feeling a little sore from the flight. I wished I knew how to use my mahier to fix the aches and pains, but I was not doing well in my studies—and not just in warrior training. "I'm going to go find some food."

She settled Jericho onto the ground and got up, dusting herself off. "Don't worry about us. He hasn't spent any mahier since he was hurt, so you don't need to bring any meat back. Just eat it all yourself, okay? You need as much of a recharge as you can get."

I nodded, then headed north, moving slower than I would have liked because of the thick jungle. Vines covered everything and there were stumps and fallen logs all over the place. I was determined, and I eventually made it out of the jungle and into a clearing.

There were two farms side-by-side. One was small, with a single ox. They probably used it to help plow their fields. The farm next to it was larger, though, and they had a pen with a bunch of animals.

As I got closer, I saw some looked like cows, but they were different from any cows I'd ever seen. They were smaller, with long fur. The ox next door would be a lot tastier, but that farm didn't look like they could afford to spare it.

Once I got close to the big animal pen, I called my dragon. The shift happened almost immediately, my multi-colored scales popping up through my skin in an instant. The cows were suddenly nervous, and started to make some noise. I didn't really want any attention, so I grabbed one between my two front legs and jumped into the air, flying back to Eva and Jericho with the thing. I ate the whole funny-looking cow all by myself in less than fifteen minutes. I had never been so hungry.

Once I picked the bones clean, it was time to get back to work. "Eva, are you ready? You're going to have to get him up on my back again."

She said she was, but it turned out she wasn't as ready as she thought. It took her ten minutes to get Jericho up, and another five to get him propped up the right way. It wasn't easy, and I hoped she hadn't hurt him even more.

Once she told me they were set, I leaped into the air again. This time, I felt stronger. Probably because I had just devoured a whole cow. I got up to the best cruising altitude fast, and from there on, the flying was easier. Up above the clouds, gliding through the thin air, it was a lot easier to keep the winds from blowing Eva and Jericho away.

We flew north like that for hours before I spotted Ellesmere Island ahead. Before I could say anything, I heard Eva shouting to let me know we were almost there. I was too tired to use my mahier for anything but the wind barrier, so Eva had to let Ochana know where we were and our situation. We made it the rest of the way by simply gliding to the island because that was about all the strength I had left. I sure couldn't have lasted another hour.

Once we landed, she dragged Jericho off my back faster than she had the first time, and she didn't fall down. I could see it took all her strength, but she laid him down as gently as she could. I staggered, my exhaustion taking over. I just didn't have any strength left. My mahier was tapped out. With so little left, I couldn't maintain my dragon and started transforming back into my human form. As soon as that was done, I fell to my knees.

Next to me, holding Jericho's head in her lap, Eva said, "A Realm of dragons is on its way. I've been using my energy to try to help Jericho, and I don't know if it did any good, but I used up most of my power, too."

I could only nod, too tired to answer her. Jericho looked even worse than I felt. His breathing had gone from steady, deep breaths to a rapid, shallow wheezing. He had a trickle of blood coming from the corner of his mouth. I tried to sense his injuries, but I didn't have enough power left in me; all I could feel was his heartbeat. That was enough to scare me, though, since it was beating as fast as a hummingbird's.

His whole body suddenly shook, and his breath rattled around in his chest, wet and bubbly. I was no doctor, but my first thought was that he had a punctured lung. I couldn't lose him now, not when help was so close. I grabbed Eva's hand and focused on pushing my energy into him, willing it to flow through him. I only needed to hold him together for a little while longer. I didn't know if it would work, but it was worth a try.

Suddenly, I felt a warm tingling in my hand where I touched Eva's. I could feel her mahier flowing into me and through me. There was only a trickle of it, but that was more than I could give him. I cleared my mind and focused on him, using both our power to try to keep him alive.

A hand grasped my shoulder gently, startling me. I looked up and saw a human with a Woland's red eyes. He said, "You did well, Keeper. We'll take it from here."

My eyes drifted around to find four other dragons. One shifted out of his human, and two others lifted Jericho onto the dragon's back. One of them followed him up onto the dragon's back and held him steady. Two more summoned their dragons, and the fifth one, the one who had put his hand on my shoulder, said, "One of you ride each of them. I can feel how empty your mahier is, Prince, but we don't have time to feed."

As Eva and I climbed aboard, Jericho's dragon mount took to the air and disappeared, along with another dragon. We were left alone on the island with our mounts. A moment later, they were in the air as well, and I could feel my dragon's muscles heaving beneath me. They were flying as fast as they could, I figured.

And then, pop. We were descending on Ochana, and I'd never been so happy to see it before. Jericho was below me, being lifted from his dragon mount. As we slowed down and banked in to land, they were putting Jericho on a stretcher, and he was whisked away. I wondered where they were taking him.

Once we landed, a blue dragon came up and bowed slightly. "Prince Colton. We are all happy to see you and the Golden Dragon safe and well."

I looked away, trying to see where they were taking Jericho.

The blue dragon nodded and said, "You're right to worry. His eyes were rolling up and he was breathing his last breath when they landed. Several of us had to use our mahier together just to keep him from passing. You saved his life, you know. The healers will do all they can, of course, and Ochana has the best in all the world. If there is any place on

Earth where he could live, this is it. You did well to bring him home."

I was too exhausted to care about anything except Jericho, so all I really heard from her speech was that he almost died and they were trying to keep him alive. That was enough to understand, for now. It was far more than I could have given him on my best day, and with this being one of the worst, I couldn't ask for much more.

Chapter Six

Eva and I waited outside Jericho's room, pacing. It felt like I'd been there for hours, and maybe I had. Some of the healers told me to get some rest. I'm sure I looked terrible after wearing myself out on that long flight to Ellesmere Island, but there was no way I'd leave Jericho until he woke up. If he even did.

My parents—Rylan and Sila, not the humans I grew up with—had come by once for about twenty minutes, and it had taken me awhile to stop being angry at them for leaving. I knew they had a kingdom to run and a war to get ready for, but part of me still felt they should be there for him, or maybe I was angry they left Eva and me here alone.

Eva must have seen my expression, because after they left, she said, "They *are* being there for him. By defending Ochana, they'll make sure he still has a kingdom to protect when he wakes up."

I gave her a nod. She was right and I knew it, so I tried to set aside my feelings. It didn't help anyone for me to stay angry about things I knew were outside anyone's control. I still kept pacing, though. It irritated Eva, but she didn't say anything. She knew I needed to keep moving so I didn't lose my mind.

An hour later, the lead healer came out of Jericho's room. She had a sour look on her face until she spotted us and put on her "doctor face"—calm and clinical. I went over to her right away, eager to hear any news. She held up her hand to stop me. "Before you hit me with a thousand questions, let me tell you what you really want to know. Councilor Jericho has several broken bones, his lungs were punctured in two places, and he had a lot of internal bleeding. We can make mahier do wondrous things to heal, but it has its limits."

"Is he dying?" I blurted, unable to stop myself before the words came out.

She shook her head. "I can't say for sure. It depends on how strong he is, and how much he wants to live. But this is Jericho we're talking about."

"If anyone can survive those injuries, he can." It was true, too, not just me trying to convince myself.

"We'll have healers working on him for as long as their mahier remains, but they have to stop and eat; they need to recharge sometimes. There's also a limit to how much we can do at once without straining his body. That would do more harm than good."

I looked down at my feet and took a deep breath. I had experienced draining all my mahier before, so I knew what she was talking about. I just didn't like it. "When will we be able to go see him?"

She gave me a faint smile and put her hand on my shoulder. Looking me in the eye, she said, "I believe we might be able to let him wake up after his current treatment is done. We have two healers in the room, working on his lungs. Once they use up all their energy, Jericho should wake up by himself shortly after. We can't be sure what condition he'll be in mentally, but like you said, if anyone can survive those injuries, he can."

The exhausted-looking healer walked away, leaving the hallway empty except for Eva and me. I knew the treatments lasted about a half an hour, having watched the healers coming and going for a while by that time. I let out a deep sigh, then went to go sit by Eva to wait it out.

She grabbed my hand. I didn't know if she was trying to comfort me, or if she needed comforting, or both. Either way, I appreciated it.

* * *

The last healer came out of Jericho's room and stopped long enough to tell us he should be awake soon, and that we should be there when he did. That was the whole reason Eva and I had been sitting there for hours, but I thanked her. Then Eva and I waited inside the bare room. Jericho lay on his bed, eyes closed, hands folded across his stomach. In one corner, his assistant was reading a book. She looked a lot like Mira, my own assistant.

She glanced up, saw that it was me, and bolted to her feet to bow.

"No," I said, "no need for that. We're all just here for Jericho. Have a seat, read your book. Pay us no mind."

There were two wooden stools next to the bed and I plopped down on one. Eva joined me on the other. It didn't take long for Jericho to stir. I had been sort of absentmindedly sensing him with my mahier to keep distracted, tracking his breathing and his heartbeat. The first thing I noticed was his pulse speeding up a little bit, and his breathing wasn't as even.

His eyelids fluttered open, and he tried to say something, but coughed instead. Eva handed him a glass of water and helped him take a few sips. The effort seemed to drain him, and he lay back and closed his eyes for a moment.

After he caught his breath, he opened his eyes again and gave Eva a quick nod. That was as much thanks as she was likely to get from him. He tried to talk again, but this time his voice was less cracked. "Pleased you're...OK, both of you... The Keepers need to be kept safe."

I smiled at him. "I'm OK, but only because of what you did. I think I owe you my life."

He shook his head faintly. "My duty. My honor...don't owe..."

Eva reached out and rested her hand on his arm. "So how does it feel to be a golf ball?"

I grinned. He really had taken quite a whack, but I wasn't sure he would get the humor. Did Wolands play golf?

"I feel like I've been run over by a steamroller," he said, some of his strength coming back to him. "But something is wrong, deep inside, something with my mahier, I can't be sure. All I know is, I have no strength."

I could tell that just by looking at him. "When will you be better? We need you. I don't think I can do this without you. I'm not ready to save the world all alone." It was awkward telling him my fears, because Jericho had no room for fear in his world, but I wasn't going to lie to him. We did need help.

He actually gave me a faint smile, which surprised me. He said, "You aren't alone. You're only one half of the Keeper of Dragons, and the other half is your true friend. You have Cairo, who would go to the ends of the Earth to protect Eva. You have your parents, who love you even though they only just met you. You have every Dragon in Ochana and every free Elf and Fairy, plus the Trolls that remain."

I forced a smile onto my face and said, "You shouldn't talk so much. You're weak and need to save your strength." He was right, though. I had three kingdoms supporting me, and my best friend. Meanwhile, Jericho was bedridden and somehow sick, and I was feeling sorry for myself. I straighten my back, sitting taller on the stool. "Of course. You're right. Now the question is, what do we do next?"

Eva blurted, "We go see the Mermaids. A fourth kingdom to help us."

I waited for him to argue with her. Instead, he closed his eyes for a moment. With my mahier sensing him, I felt his exhaustion. "I know there's no stopping the Golden Dragon, no matter what I say, as long as I'm here in bed. She'll convince you to go to the Mermaids, and you'll follow her. Too tired to fight, so I'm just going to go with it. Maybe she's right. I doubt it, but I hope I'm wrong."

Eva grinned and gave him a wink, even though his eyes were still closed. She said, "Well, you're right about that. So, where do we find them?"

He coughed, a wet and raspy sound. It didn't seem as bad as it had before, but I could hear the fluid in his lungs.

When his coughing eased, he said, "You'll find them in the Dead Sea. Trust the Fates. If you're meant to find them, you will. We haven't spoken to them in a long time, and I have no idea how you'll be received. Their leader is Queen Desla. Find her, tell her what's at stake."

Eva nodded, enthusiastic. "Thank you. I just have this feeling that we're meant to go there. I couldn't tell you why."

He didn't reply, and I thought maybe he had passed out again. Then he opened his eyes and looked right at me. "One more thing. In their kingdom grows a certain plant. Whatever this is that I feel deep within me, it might help me. If you can, get a handful of that. Queen Desla will know of the plant. I might be able to do without it, but I just feel so weak. Not sure I have the strength, even with the help of the healers. I only wish we'd known of this plant for your Uncle Jago." Jericho's voice trailed off.

I clenched my fist and nodded. "I'll get that weed, no matter what. I'll make them give it to me." I glanced at Eva, who looked at me oddly. Maybe she didn't understand my determination. The Farros had killed my uncle and now the Carnites might kill Jericho. All because of Eldrick.

Jericho's heart slowed down a bit and his breathing became slow and steady.

"He's gone back to sleep."

Eva patted his arm and said, "Let him sleep. He needs all the rest he can get. Come on, let's go. We need to get ready for a long trip, then you need to say goodbye to your parents."

* * *

After we left Jericho, Eva went to her room to bathe and change while I went to go find my parents.

In the middle of all this, I didn't know if I would see the king and queen again. Maybe I hadn't grown up with them, but they were still my parents. I knew they loved me anyway. In a way, I loved them too, even though I didn't know them. There was a sort of bond in being related by blood.

I found Rylan in the throne room at the head of a line of assistants with papers for him to read and sign. Being the king didn't look like a lot of fun.

As I entered, his eyes locked on mine and he smiled. "Colton, my son. It is so good to see you. Come sit next to me, let's talk."

I walked up the steps to the platform and sat on the smaller throne to Rylan's right. The king waved the assistants away. They made their way to the back of the throne room, giving us our privacy.

"How is Jericho?" Rylan asked. "I haven't had time to go visit him in hours."

I squirmed a little in the uncomfortable throne. No matter how I shifted, I couldn't quite get settled in. My whole life was kind of like that now.

"He's still badly wounded, and he seems to have some sort sickness; he thinks it's his mahier. The healers' mahier isn't curing it, something about how he's reached the limits of how much the healers can help him. If they keep pouring mahier into him, it will do more harm than good."

Rylan looked up at the ceiling for a moment, and he looked troubled. "I see. So then, whether he recovers depends mostly on how strong he is. It's a good thing that if anyone is strong enough, our friend Jericho is."

My father didn't sound convinced. Maybe the news I brought would help him deal with it better. Or maybe he'd refuse to let Eva and me go. I decided I would go anyway, if that's where Eva went, but I had to tell him our plans.

I took a deep breath, then said, "Eva and I are going to the Dead Sea to bring the Mermaids into the Elven Alliance. The good news is that some sort of special plant grows in the Mermaid kingdom, and Jericho says it could heal him. I just need to grab a handful while we're there, and then the healers can do the rest."

Rylan nodded and gave me a faint smile. "Yes, I think I know the one you mean. It's the one that has more yellow than green, and grows on a stalk like kelp, but I forget the name." Rylan closed his eyes and sighed. "I am told if we had known of such plant, it may have saved my brother." Rylan's eyes flashed open and studied me. "Going to the Mermaids would not have been my first choice, but if the Keeper of Dragons have both decided that's the best course, then I'll leave it to fate. You're destined to drive back the Time of Fear. Whatever you two do together, things will happen the way they're meant to. Who am I to get in the way of that?"

That was surprising. I had figured he'd demand we go to Greece, or maybe some other plan I hadn't thought of. The trust he put in me made me think of my nightmare, where everyone cheered at me and believed I would succeed, even while the darkness was coming for them.

I shoved that thought away. If I dwelled on it too much, I might freeze up and do nothing at all. Whether going to see the Mermaids was the best plan or not, it was still better than just sitting in Ochana, waiting for the end to come. I said, "Eva and I are leaving right away. We'll head back to Paraiso first, pick up Cairo and Realm Five, then go east to meet the Mermaids."

He let out a long breath, like all the fight had left him. I suppose he was afraid of losing me, yet the whole world depended on him letting me go. In a way, I was glad my real parents—the ones I grew up with—didn't have to know about what I was doing. I missed them so much, and I know they would have feared for me greatly.

He said, "Then I suppose you had better get going, my son. Your mother's heart and mine go with you. I'm afraid for you, but I know this is what you were born to do, you and Eva both. I just wish this hadn't happened in your lifetime. Sila is sad she hasn't had time to get to know you better since you came back to us."

Then he stood and faced me, so I got up, too. I was kind of surprised when he leaned forward and gave me a quick hug instead of putting his hand on my shoulder or shaking my hand, like he usually did. He must have been really afraid for me, and Jericho getting hurt couldn't have helped him feel better about it. When I came back with those leaves for

Jericho, and he got better, maybe Rylan would feel better, too. I smiled at the thought, and he smiled back at me. Then it was time to go.

* * *

After stopping at another farm along the African coast to eat, Eva and I landed back in Paraiso to gather up Cairo and Realm Five before heading east. Now that the decision had been made to go see the Mermaids, I was kind of excited. It wasn't very long ago that I thought Mermaids didn't exist. Neither did dragons, or Elves.

We both shifted back into our humans as we landed. I was getting much better at it, and could usually do it in the blink of an eye, now.

"Let's go find Cairo," Eva said.

I grinned. I had no idea why Cairo didn't want to tell her he thought they were soulmates, because to me, it was pretty obvious she felt the same way, even without knowing about the weird, magic soul-bonding thing Cairo thought it was.

She said, "What? Don't smile at me like that. You know he and I have just gotten close since I got here. I mean, we work together every day. It's only natural."

I shrugged and smirked. "I didn't say a word."

Eva rolled her eyes and I fought the urge to laugh.

A new voice to my right shouted, "Eva, Prince Colton. I'm so glad you two made it back. How is Jericho?"

I looked down at the ground. It was good to see Cairo again, but I really didn't want to have to tell him about Jericho.

Thankfully, Eva answered before it got awkward. "The healers brought him through the worst of his danger, at least for the moment. He says he feels some sort of sickness, with his mahier. He also gave us his blessing to try to recruit the Mermaids. I know it wasn't his first choice, but with him bedridden, he knew he couldn't stop us. Plus, there's a plant that grows there he asked us to gather for him."

I added, "Get the dragons ready to fly out. We'll head east again just as soon as Eva and I get something to eat. We only ate enough along the way for us to get here safely."

Cairo nodded, then waved over a Woland and told her to make sure we got all the food we needed. He said, "Food is on the way. Now, then... I thought the plan was to head to Greece where the rest of the Fairies are. Just because Jericho can't get out of bed doesn't mean he was wrong."

Eva glared at him and said, "Oh, so you don't believe he gave us his blessing? I would have thought you out of everyone here would trust me. Well, Mister Thinks-He-Knows-Everything, I guess you didn't get the memo. Jericho said we should go after the Mermaids, which you would know if you had been at your friend's side when he woke up. Like we were."

Cairo stood his ground. He looked her in the eye and said, "Someone as badly hurt as Jericho might say just about anything in that condition. And you're being unfair—you know perfectly well that I was here doing my job. I'm always doing my job. I sided with you earlier about going to the Mermaids. You had a good point, but Jericho was right. We can't waste our resources chasing the Mermaids."

Both Eva and Cairo stood tall, backs straight and fists clenched. It was clear neither was going to back down. Emotions were running high with everything that had happened recently and it seemed both were ready to take their frustration out on the other. Hoping to stop the standoff, I said, "Actually, Jericho did say that. It was something along the lines of, since he couldn't stop us from going, then he wished us luck and put his support behind us. Behind Eva, actually, because I still think we need to head north. I'm telling you, my dream—"

Eva clenched her fists tighter and yelled in frustration, glaring back and forth between Cairo and me.

Not backing down, Cairo said, "I know you're mad, but listen to reason. We need to go after the Carnites. They're going to be the easiest ones to find out of all our enemies, and they might lead us to a clue on King Eldrick's location, or even where the Elves and Trolls are being held."

I snarled, "You can't cut me off and then ignore what I said. I'm telling you, as the Keeper of Dragons, we need to head north. I don't see why we're even arguing about this. That's where the Elves and Trolls are." And since when were we planning on chasing the Carnites?

Eva gave us each a final glare and then turned on her heels to walk away.

Cairo and I both looked after her in disbelief.

Over her shoulder, she said, "When you two are done arguing with each other and ignoring what I have the say, then we'll talk, but I'm not going to let you treat me like this. I'm going to get something to eat, and you two can beat the snot out of each other for all I care."

She let out a shout of frustration and stormed back toward the dragon encampment in Paraiso. Cairo and I watched her leave, and I realized my jaw had dropped. I snapped my mouth shut and looked at Cairo.

He looked back at me and shrugged helplessly. "I can't believe she was so mad at us. I mean, it's just one little disagreement, right? We'd have figured it out eventually."

I could only shake my head at him. He didn't know Eva the way I did. She never just walked away from any fight, unless she was really angry and had enough. "Actually, I think you're on thin ice with her. Trust me on this. Eva is way angrier than you think, and she can hold a grudge when she wants to."

I let out a deep sigh, letting my frustration flow away. She was my best friend, but she was making a mistake, and Cairo was letting her. I added, "If you honestly believe that stuff you said about being her *Vera Salit*, I think you need to go and apologize, whether you think you did anything wrong or not. Seriously, this is the time to tell her you believe that you two are soulmates. If you don't, things might really get away from you. I wouldn't leave it to chance like that."

Cairo's eyes flared, flashing red. His whole body stiffened and he stood straighter, it was clear I had stepped over some invisible line in the sand. He said, "I'm not ready for that. This isn't the right time. You think you're the only one who knows her? I don't think you give her enough credit, Cole. Anyway, it's between me and her whether we're soulmates. It has nothing to do with you. With all due respect, you need to back off and leave me alone right now. If you want to stay here and follow me around arguing, whatever happens will be on your hands."

I couldn't believe what I just heard. I didn't think he would really hurt me, but he was definitely ready to take a swing. I had no idea what would happen to him if he did, considering that I'm the Prince of Ochana and the Keeper of Dragons. I didn't want to find out. No matter how mad I was at him at the moment, he was a good dragon and loyal to Ochana, and I didn't want anything to happen to him.

So, I turned around and walked away, fuming. I swore that later, after we had both cooled off a bit, Cairo and I were going to have a long talk and straighten things out between us, one way or another.

Chapter Seven

I looked down on the small room almost as though I floated above it. King Eldrick stood over someone sitting in a chair, but I couldn't see who it was. Eldrick blocked my view.

"I promise you, the pain will end when you tell me what I want to know." Eldrick's voice sounded like he had a sneer on his face.

"I'll tell you nothing. Not because of who he is, but because of who you are." The voice sounded familiar, and it only took a moment to realize it was the Elven Princess Clara, Gaber's sister.

Eldrick stepped around behind her, and I could finally see both of their faces. He said, "I don't see why you protect him. After all these years, you don't owe him anything. He's certainly not out there looking for you, Clara. He's back in Ochana, doing nothing."

She shook her head and glared. "Someone is looking for me. I sense it, and when they find me, your time will be done, traitor."

He laughed and said, "That's a good one. You call me a traitor? The king and queen were traitors to their race. I tried to make us strong, the strongest of them all, and for my efforts..."

"They exiled you, even though your crime deserved death. You were only spared because you're part of our family, or you were until you came back and killed our parents. Tell me, Eldrick, how does killing two of the five originals make my race stronger?"

Eldrick's grip on the chair back tightened, his knuckles turning white from the force, but his voice sounded calm as he said, "Our race, not yours. And that's water under the bridge. I can't change the past, nor can you. But we can still look to the future."

She snarled, "There is no future in dishonor."

He ignored her. "Being crushed by a Carnite should have done it, yet he lives. Tell me how to kill him and I'll let you free to go rejoin your brother. I'll keep all of our cousins here as collateral, but the pain will stop. Think about it, Clara, you can choose right now to go free and end their suffering, or you can keep protecting a dragon, not even one of us. You two were over a long time ago. I promise you'll be OK. You don't owe him anything."

Clara snarled back at him, "You want me turn to the darkness just like you and your followers did. Never! Elves are strongest when we embrace our nature, our Truth. I'll never help you, no matter what it costs us."

Eldrick laughed and reached out to a table that I couldn't see well. When he drew his hand back, he carried a small, wicked knife. "I would say this isn't going to hurt, but that would be a lie. Are you ready?"

I sat bolt upright in bed, Clara's screams echoing in my ears. I was covered in sweat and shivered in the cold night air. Why did I keep having these dreams? I didn't know what they all meant, and had a feeling I was missing some part of a bigger picture. I didn't think they were really dreams at all. They felt real.

I decided to go for an early morning walk to calm myself down a bit, and threw on my clothes before walking outside. I blinked down to the jungle floor, then strolled toward the Elves' mystical lake with my head down, lost in thought about the dreams.

Before I ever made it to the lakeshore, I heard a loud bang. I stopped and listened, trying not to even breathe so I could hear well. There were some rustling noises, and I walked toward them. In a small clearing at the jungle's edge, just outside of Paraiso, Cairo was stuffing supplies into a backpack. Was he leaving? What could make a dragon like him abandon his duty? He was supposed to be here protecting Eva.

"Tell me you aren't just running away, Cairo. I'd be mighty disappointed, and I think Eva would, too." I clenched my jaw and stared at him, angry and ready to take a swing. "Tell me why you're running away now, when we all need you most."

He looked up, startled. It seemed he hadn't heard me approaching. "I'm not running away. I'm a bit offended you would think that. The truth is, Eva left in the middle of the night to go find the Mermaids without us. I guess she got tired of waiting. I'm going to go find her—she's not safe out there alone, and we can't risk losing the Golden Dragon."

My jaw dropped. How could she do that? She knew how dangerous it was out there. Then again, she always was the braver of us. Well, I couldn't let Cairo go alone, not when he was determined to go out and find Eva himself. And something told me he wouldn't wait for me to gather a team to help track Eva.

I took a deep breath, shoved my anger aside, and said, "We have to find her. We should work together. We'll be safer together than apart."

He nodded and said, "Ten minutes." Then he began stuffing things back into his backpack.

I blinked back up to my room and grabbed my own pack. I had never unpacked it, so I just slung it over my shoulder. A couple minutes later, I was back with Cairo.

He gave me a nod, then turned and began walking east. "My senses tell me she was walking. I don't know why she didn't fly, but we can't just turn into our dragons. I'd lose track of her from the air."

I frowned. That meant it would take longer to find her, if we could even catch up to her. "Are you sure you'll be able to find her? How?"

Cairo said, "I told you, we are soulmates. *Vera Salit* can use our mahier to reach out and sense our soulmate's direction. When we get close to her, I'll be able to feel it more clearly. But like I said, if we fly, we'll be moving too quickly and I'll lose her path."

Together, we moved away from Paraiso and deeper into the jungle. We walked for the rest of that morning, stopped for a quick lunch of berries and plants we'd gathered along the way, then continued on. The hours ticked by. From the occasional glimpses of the sun overhead through the jungle canopy, I guessed it to be about four o'clock.

As we reached the top of a small hill and began walking down, headed ever eastward, I sensed something. I had my mahier pushed outward, hoping I could sense any danger or humans we came across before we were seen. I said, "Stop. There's something dark nearby, and it's heading our way.

No, wait, there's more than one. Five, seven... Ten. I count ten of them."

Cairo's head whipped around as he looked for any danger. "How far away are they, and what are they?"

Suddenly, my senses reeled. Whatever was out there, they were powerful. And familiar.

J.A. Culican

Chapter Eight

"Elden. Ten of them, a few hundred yards away and coming on fast. They're almost on us," I muttered as I concentrated on the Elden.

He said in a half-whisper, "Elden? We have to hide. There's no way we can win against ten of them."

I didn't need to be told twice. The Elden must have known where we were somehow, because the odds of them coming straight at us were just too small. I felt fear rising up in my belly.

I looked around, desperate to find a place to hide from the approaching Elden, but there was nowhere that looked good enough. But if they knew where we were, there was no use in hiding anyway. Not here.

To our east, something moved. A quick glance told me it was the Elden reaching the top of a small hill. One of them pointed at us.

I looked at Cairo. "Too late, they found us."

His eyes widened, just for a split second, and he said, "Run."

Once again, we found ourselves running for our lives. There was no way we could beat so many of them, and in the back of my mind, I wondered where they had come from. I wish I knew how they'd found us.

We ran as fast as we could, our mahier helping give us energy. I really wanted to ask why we didn't just turn into dragons and fly away, but Cairo was an experienced Woland. If he didn't shift, it must've been for a good reason. I shoved that thought aside and focused on running.

We bolted down a little path between two low, rolling hills. I realized we were trying to stay out of sight as much as possible while we ran. Then, up ahead about fifty feet, a pair of Elden came into view. Their black, beady eyes and razor-sharp teeth zeroed in on us and they charged.

Cairo slowed and pulled his sword, so I did the same, but we didn't stop. Side-by-side, we crashed into the two scouts. There was a quick flash of blades as Cairo defeated one and I held off the other. Then he dealt with the one attacking me.

"Come on, we have to get out of here," he half-shouted before putting his sword away and sprinting north again.

I was hot on his heels. We kept moving long past the point I should've been exhausted. I found it easier to use my tilium to keep the fatigue away, but Cairo wasn't having any problem keeping up using mahier. It was an odd thing to think about at that moment.

An arrow streaked past my face and I almost missed a step. Cairo shouted to keep going, so I did. I put my head down and ran as fast as I could.

We rounded another hill and up ahead, a forest stretched into the distance. My heart leaped for joy. All we had to do was get to the tree line and we might be able to lose our pursuers. Cairo saw it, too, because he changed direction to head directly at it. The minutes passed as the forest came closer and closer, but there were no more arrows flying by. I didn't look back to check, but I figured the Elden decided they could run faster without trying to shoot us. Once they closed the distance or chased us into exhaustion, they'd have plenty of time to shoot us. It was not a pleasant thought.

One instant, we were running through open rolling plains, probably visible for miles, and then we burst through the tree line. Hah! Let them try to shoot us running through that thick jungle.

My tilium was slowly draining. I knew it wouldn't last forever, and I figured the Elden had more of it than I did. When I ran out, I would be able to switch to my mahier, but Cairo would just be out of power. I couldn't leave him behind, so I'd have to stop, and we'd have to fight the Elden alone whether he had any mahier left or not.

That seemed like a bad idea so I said, "We have to hide. They'll outrun us eventually."

"You're right. Follow me."

There wasn't time to ask questions, so I just followed him through the forest, jumping over logs and dodging branches as best we could. The twigs and branches still left scratches and cuts on my face and arms. I noticed he was running us right at a large clump of fallen trees that formed a huge bramble. I really hoped he was going to go around it, but no such luck.

He shouted, "Hide in there." Then he jumped, and when he landed, he slid into that big cluster like he was sliding into home plate. I did the same. "Give me your hand," he said.

Before I could reach out, he snatched my hand in his and closed his eyes. I could feel his power surging, just like I could feel mine being drained. Whatever he was doing, I hoped it would work.

Not far behind us, I could hear the Elden scrambling and shouting as they crashed through the woods. They were coming through the trees like hunters, spread out to find us. All of a sudden, one stopped and shouted. The others stopped, too, gathering around him.

A second later, he pointed west, to the right of where I lay hidden in the brambles. The whole troop ran off in that direction. They seemed to think they were hot on our trail from the way they were carrying on. Then their voices faded with distance.

When I decided they would be out of earshot, I looked at Cairo and raised one eyebrow. I didn't know what he had done, but I was sure curious. He had his eyes closed, and I waited like that minute after minute. I started counting my heartbeats, just to have something to focus on and take away the fear. About four minutes later, he opened his eyes and grinned at me.

"What did you do?" I asked.

"I made every tree in the forest look like us," he said. "It sure confused them, but when I started letting go of the disguise in different parts of the forest, it made it look like we were running west. Then when our little hiding spot was going to be the only place around here that still showed 'us' to their powers, I used your energy to make us seem like trees. They could've seen right through it if they were close enough, but they were tracking us with their tilium, not their eyes. I don't know how they were following us."

That was incredible. "So you mean to say, we look like trees to them right now?"

He smirked and seemed awfully full of himself over the whole thing. Although I had to admit it was pretty clever. I grinned back at him.

He said, "They're running west, so we should head east."

"Yeah, that was the way we were going, right? I don't think that's changed. So I guess it's a good thing you sent them west."

He chuckled, and we climbed out from under the brambles. For the next few miles, as we walked fast to the east, he still kept hold of my hand. It slowed us down, but I could feel him still using my energy. He was probably still luring those Elden away from us, so I didn't mind.

After a few miles, he let go of my hand; I suddenly felt how low my mahier was. I sensed his power had been mostly drained, too. We walked in silence, trying to slowly absorb more mahier and recharge a bit. I was sure we would need it again, probably sooner than I wanted. Only a big meal of meat would let us recharge quickly, though.

We finally came to the end of that stretch of jungle and stepped back out into the bright light of day. This time, there were no gentle hills, only flatlands. It was kind of scary looking, or depressing. Maybe both. We kept walking.

A few hours after that, we dove back into another jungle. This one wasn't as thick as the last one had been, and it didn't look like it was quite as large, but the sun was ready to go down soon. "Maybe we should make camp here," I said. "The trees will give us some cover, and if anymore Elden come along, it will give us something for you to disguise us with."

He nodded. "Good idea. After you, my prince." He held his hand out toward the forest. Once we were fairly deep inside the woods, we made camp. Cairo used his dragon breath to start a fire, I couldn't wait to have control of mine. It burned low and slow, and I hoped it wouldn't give away our position, but the forest was damp. I figured it would get pretty cold at night. Getting hypothermia wouldn't help our mission, so it was worth Cairo spending that little bit of energy. Besides, as we slept, our power would recharge.

As the daylight went away and darkness fell, we cooked a couple of rabbits Cairo had caught. We set them up on spits to cook over low flames, slowly turning them by hand while we chatted about Eva, Jericho, and so many other things. I didn't know why we both felt the need to fill the silence. Maybe we were both just scared and trying to distract ourselves, but we ended up talking more in that couple of hours than we ever had before.

After one of the inevitable lulls in conversation, he looked at me intently.

"What? Do I have some rabbit on my face?"

After a pause, he said, "How do they keep following us? That's what I want to know. I didn't mention it to you, but when we were going through the jungle earlier, there were a couple of times where I had to use my power to hide us from different patrols. They all seem to be heading in whatever direction I made the jungle illusion look like we went. I keep expecting Elden or Carnites to pop up right in front of us. You can bet I'm going to sleep with one eye open. Whether I'm watching for Elden, or watching you, I haven't decided yet."

I cocked my head. "I don't think you really need to watch me. What makes you think I have something to do with that?"

"Simple. It didn't happen until you and I were alone together. Maybe you brought the Carnites that almost killed Jericho, for all I know."

"You know I would never do that. Why would I? I've been fighting them every step of the way, and you know it." I was starting to get angry at him. It definitely hurt my feelings, and my natural reaction to that was to get mad. I didn't think I could get to the Mermaids and Eva by myself, though, so I bit my tongue. It was hard not to say everything else that was on my mind, especially after the friendliest chat we'd ever had before.

"The only thing I do know is that they're following us. Not just one group, but several. That means they're coming from farther out than I can push my senses. And that means..."

"That means that either they planted something on one of us that they can track from a long way away, or one of us is reaching out to tell them where we're at. Is that what you're going to say?"

Cairo let out a deep breath and seemed suddenly very interested in his hands. He stared at them as he said, "Yes that pretty much sums it up. The thing is,

I don't really think you're a traitor. You're the Keeper of Dragons, after all. If you're a traitor, then the whole world is doomed. I don't want to believe that."

There was no point answering him. If he thought I was a traitor, he wouldn't trust me anyway, and if he didn't think so, then I didn't know any more than he did. I looked up through the trees and into the sky, taking a deep breath. The forest smelled wonderful. If the Elden won, then simple pleasures like this would probably be gone soon. That was depressing, so I decided to think of other things. Like how we were going to get through the night without being tracked.

"Cairo, will you show me how to do your trick where you disguised us as trees back there in the jungle? That way we can sleep in shifts, and you won't be completely drained by morning."

It didn't take long for him to show me how to do it. It seemed simple enough, and like everything with mahier, it involved simple willpower more than anything else.

I decided to take first watch and let him get some sleep. He needed it more than me. It was really boring, but that was a good thing. Boredom meant our hunters weren't trying to kill us at that moment. I was also relieved. The fact that Cairo let me take first watch meant that deep down, he knew he could trust me.

Halfway through the night, I woke Cairo. When I was sure he was fully awake, I lay down on the soft forest floor, using my elbow as a pillow, and dozed off into an uneasy sleep.

* * *

The next morning, Cairo greeted me with a couple of eggs cooking on a hot rock and some sort of a flat, dry biscuit he made with some cornmeal from his little backpack. I was practically starving. It wasn't much food, but at least he shared. I couldn't ask for more than that. It wasn't like there was a convenience store anywhere out here in an African jungle, after all.

We gathered up our things and headed east again. We were making good time toward the Dead Sea. I figured Eva had probably already arrived and was talking to the Mermaids without me. I was a little sad at the thought. The idea of meeting real Mermaids was kind of exciting.

During our walk, we had to hide twice, but it was easy to avoid being spotted. Since Cairo had taught me the trick of looking like trees to their tilium senses, it got easier each time I tried to do it. Now, I barely used any power.

After that, there was more walking. Anyone who said walking wasn't great exercise had never done it like we did that day. It wasn't like walking on a road, where everything was flat and level. Walking cross-country was totally different, and every step meant we had to climb, duck, sidestep, or push through something. Every step was tiring. Thankfully, I had my mahier and tilium to keep me energized and alert.

We finally reached low, rolling hills again, and the walking became a little harder, but it became a lot easier to hide us. That's what Cairo said, anyway. He kept busy camouflaging us while I pushed my senses outward, trying to sense any threats coming in our direction.

I stopped suddenly, by reflex, and planted my hand on Cairo's chest. My body had reacted before my mind registered the threat, but it only took half a second for me to realize what it was. Something bad was in the valley on the far side of the hill we were climbing—something big and evil. "Carnites," I whispered hoarsely.

Cairo grabbed me by the front of my shirt and hit the ground, dragging me down with him. He nodded toward the top of the hill, then turned and began to slither on his belly. I followed. It took maybe twenty minutes to get to the top, but when we did, my jaw dropped. Down in the valley between three different low hills was a group of huge Carnites sitting around, talking.

And in the center, I saw a familiar face. Eva! She had been captured.

Next to me, I heard Cairo whisper, "Oh no."

My thought exactly.

Chapter Nine

I could practically feel Cairo tensing up. He said, "No! This can't be happening. We have to rescue her." He started to scramble to his feet.

I realized he was about to rush in to try to save Eva from the Carnites. We'd never save her once they knew we were there. As he rose, I wrapped my arms around his waist and locked my hands together, then used my whole weight to drag him back down to the ground.

"Be smart!" I hissed. When he struggled again, I squeezed even harder, hoping to knock the wind out of him. "Yes, we have to rescue her. You won't do it by rushing in and trying to fight three Carnites by yourself. You'll only get her killed, and you with her. I won't let you do it." I was gasping from the effort of trying to hold him down.

After a couple of seconds of struggling, he said, "Cole, let me go. You're going to give away our position." His face was turning red as he tried to get out of my grasp.

"Then stop fighting me. We have to talk about this. The Carnites don't know we're here. We can surprise them, but only if you don't rush off and do something stupid."

A couple of seconds later, he relaxed. Hesitantly, I released him, but I didn't unlock my grip.

No longer resisting, Cairo said, "Okay. Thanks. I know you're right, but I will not just leave her in there. I—"

"Shhh," I hissed. I wanted to hear what the Carnites were saying, but I couldn't make it out over him talking.

He snapped his mouth shut, then turned his head to try to listen with me.

"... are you going? Who are you, little human?" one Carnite said.

"Who cares who she is? Meat on bones, meat in mouth. We should eat the tasty morsel."

The first Carnite smacked the second one across the back of its head. "You are too stupider. How she see us? She not a morsel, no, she maybe a dragon?"

Eva looked at it right in the eyes, and even from where Cairo and I were hiding, I could see that her helpless, scared expression was faked. That was Eva, always keeping her head on straight and looking for the opportunities. She said, "What's a dragon? There's no such thing as dragons, everyone knows that."

The Carnite looked doubtful. He said, "If you not a dragon, why you in the jungle? Where you village? Why you see us?"

Eva shrugged. Her crisp, clear voice carried to our ears easily. "You ask a lot of questions. I'm just a helpless human, walking in the jungle for the same reason you are, I bet. I was gathering Lilacost; they're perfect for the flower arrangements we make back in my village. It's just north of here."

The second Carnite scratched its head, then after a second, said, "What's a Lilacost?"

Eva kept her face perfectly straight, from what I saw from my hiding spot, and said, "About twenty bucks, if it's arranged well."

I groaned inside. She was caught by Carnites and surrounded, and she was making jokes? Part of me envied her courage, and the other part of me wanted her to be quiet before she got herself killed. I whispered, "I don't think we have much time. Got any ideas?"

Cairo got back up to his hands and knees and looked at Eva. He was very quiet for a few moments, then said, "Actually, I do. If we're going to save her, we need two things. First, a distraction. Then, a way to slow the Carnites down after we grab her."

That made sense. Better yet, it was pretty simple. Now the only question was how to do the two things. I remembered how he had lured away the Elden in the jungle, and thought that might work again. Especially since the Carnites weren't the brightest creatures on Earth. "Okay. You can do that trick where you make every tree look and smell like us, right? So if you handle that, and I handle the distraction, we might be able to do this."

Cairo nodded. It was about as good of a plan as we could get, at least in the time we had available. He was about to say something but I held up my hand to shush him. the Carnites were talking again.

"The morsel lies. I never see no Lilacosts here. No bucks, too. How we get truth from it?"

The other Carnite, the one who'd been smacked, shrugged its giant shoulders. "They could be real. Maybe new name for old thing. I bet King Eldrick would know." Then it chuckled, and the sound sent a shiver down my spine. "And he use his strong powers, gets the truth for us."

Eva let out a little chirp of shock. She blurted, "You work for King Eldrick? You know you can't trust him, right? Whatever he promised you, it's a lie."

The first Carnite shook its head. "No. King Eldrick make promise. We work for him, we work for promise."

Eva shook her head. "You're making a mistake, I promise you. What did he say he'd give you? It can't be worth being his slave."

The two Carnites began to argue amongst themselves, and I couldn't tell what they were saying anymore. Their accent was just too thick when they were angry. They were shoving each other back and forth. I hoped they would get in a fight, giving us the distraction we were looking for, but I didn't count on it. I kept trying to think of other options.

In a couple of seconds, however, they settled down. Then the second one told Eva, "Eldrick promise Carnites their own home. A Carnite king. Carnites get all of the Congo, new Carnite homeland. We get a home, just like stupid Elves, stupid Trolls. All we have to do is help him get rid of dragons."

I filed that away, hoping it might be useful later. At least now we knew what the Carnites were doing and that their attacks were directed, not random. We suspected it before, but now we could be sure.

Cairo whispered, "Now they have a plan—taking Eva to King Eldrick. We can't let that happen. We can't let them split up the Keeper of Dragons, Cole."

He was right, but we still needed that distraction. I had an idea, though. I remembered the brilliant light that came from the mahier ropes the dragons had used when they rescued me and Eva from the Carnites the last time. I wondered if we could use it to tie their ankles together. Big Carnites would probably fall hard, right? At least, that was my idea.

I told Cairo, and he didn't look enthusiastic, but he hadn't come up with any ideas of his own yet.

I heard Eva say, "Where are the Elves and Trolls? You helped get rid of them, right? If you didn't, he wouldn't give you the Congo, so I bet you did help. Where did he take them? Or didn't he tell you."

The first Carnite sat up straighter, lifting his chin in the air as he said, "King Eldrick tell us. We took Elves there. Took Trolls there." Then it leaned forward until his face was only a foot from Eva's and said loudly, "But we not tell you, little morsel. Fake village girl. You think we stupid, but we not."

Eva said, "I don't think you're stupid. I think you're very smart to want your own homeland. People must underestimate you all the time, right? King Eldrick did. He got you to help him, even with no guarantee he would give you the Congo. He must think you're really dumb." She shook her head slowly, looking sympathetic.

Cairo whispered to me, "That idea could work, but do you know how to do it? Binding things with your mahier takes a lot of energy."

At least this concern, I had an answer to. "No, I don't how to do it with my mahier. Fortunately for us, though, I'm a lot better at controlling my tilium. I bet I can do something like it with the Farro energy I took."

"I'm not a betting dragon, but it looks like we don't have much of a choice. You think you can do it, so I guess we'll have to try. It's just too bad you're betting on Eva's life at the same time."

He was right. I was betting I could do it with my tilium, and if I failed, she'd be gone or dead. Still, I felt reasonably confident that I could make it happen, and what other choice did I have? I couldn't think of any.

One Carnite said, "Enough. Tasty morsel think she can fool Carnites. Everyone think Carnites stupid."

Oh great, now they were repeating themselves.

It continued, "We smart enough to take dragon girl to King Eldrick. We smart enough to know, you not village girl."

It had practically shouted that last sentence, and as it sat on its knees, it began to bounce up and down, smashing its tree club into the dirt next to it and crying out a deep, animal grunting, like what I imagined gorillas would do when they were excited.

"Cairo, we've got to do something right now. As soon as I manifest the bindings, you create the illusion. Can you make it sound like someone is crashing through the bushes just south of us?"

He raised one eyebrow and nodded, and I guessed he hadn't thought of it himself. The Carnites would chase that noise, hopefully, leading them away from Eva. It was worth a shot.

I closed my eyes and focused on bringing out my tilium. I willed it to stretch from my hands and fingers out toward the Carnites. As it went farther and farther, it got thinner and thinner, going from a cone to a tight focus, looking like a rope. I made it slither across the jungle floor and, when it reached them, I had it wind in and out between their ankles. I tied it in knots as it went. The Carnites would be in for a rude surprise when they started chasing the distraction.

Then, using my mahier, I pushed outward with my mind until it enveloped all three Carnites. I focused on putting thoughts into their heads. I wanted it to sound like a scream coming from behind them when I alerted them that we were here.

I felt my mahier sliding into their heads fairly easily. I didn't think I could've controlled them, or done anything super exciting while I was inside their heads; I had a feeling that their stupidity somehow protected them from the worst of what a dragon could do, not that I knew how to do the worst.

I took a deep breath and then mentally screamed the words into their heads, "Elves, Trolls, they're coming to take the girl, they want the reward for themselves!"

In an instant, all three Carnites were standing, looking around. Then they heard the phantom sounds of people crashing around in the bushes to the south. The first two, who had been arguing, moved faster than I thought possible as they tried to run after the noise. I would sure hate to try to outrun those things without a good head start.

Halfway through their steps, my tilium rope went tight and they crashed to the ground. I could feel the ground shake, even from that distance, and the noise was terrible.

Only one problem—the third Carnite hadn't left with the others. It had stayed with Eva.

I said, "Go get her." Then I focused on stretching out my tilium again, going back over their ankles and weaving the two threads together to make them stronger. Then I yanked my hands back, drawing the tilium ropes tight.

Cairo sprinted toward the third Carnite, and although it saw the movement coming out of the jungle, it didn't seem to be able to make sense of what it was seeing. It stared at Cairo dumbly until almost the last second. When Cairo was five feet away, he leaped into the air and swung his sword over his head with both hands, bringing it down on the Carnite's skull. Eva jumped to her feet and ran back the way Cairo had come, heading toward me.

I threw my hand out, shooting a tilium rope at the third one's tree trunk club. It wrapped around it, and the club slowed, but it didn't stop. It snapped my tilium rope in half, but slowing it down had been enough; Cairo dove out of the way.

I drew my sword and rushed out into the open area between my hiding spot and where they had been questioning Eva. I ran right at that third Carnite, passing Eva going the other way. I didn't have time to worry about what she was doing. The Carnite tried to raise its club again, but it was too slow. I ran by and swung my sword as hard as I could one-handed, and felt it bite deep into the creature's gut.

I turned and saw that Cairo hadn't slowed down when he dodged the club. He kept running, and then jumped onto the two bound Carnites. From the dirt, the two simply stared, apparently not believing their own eyes. In moments, Cairo had ended their threat permanently.

Eva came walking back into the clearing, looking around and nodding as though impressed. I wanted to yell at her, shout at her for leaving in the middle of the night without telling anyone, but we didn't have time. The Carnite I had cut was badly wounded, and if we wanted to get any information from it, we had to ask quickly.

We didn't ask fast enough, though. It didn't get the chance to say anything before it died, joining its two friends wherever Carnites went when they died.

I looked at Cairo and said, "That wasn't quite the plan, but it worked. I'm sorry we couldn't get this one to talk before it died."

He shrugged and said, "I'm sorry, too, but that's the way of war."

J.A. Culican

Chapter Ten

Cairo leaned on his sword, catching his breath. He glanced up at Eva, and his face turned even redder than usual. I understood just how he felt, too. She almost got herself killed, and us. None of the Carnites were still alive, so most of our questions were still unanswered.

Eva looked at him for a couple of seconds, then exploded. "What are you looking at?"

I couldn't tell if it was a challenge or a real question, but it made him stand bolt upright. He waved his hand to show the jungle around us and shouted, "You shouldn't have run off like that. How could you just get up and leave without telling anyone? Don't you know—"

She cut him off, shouting back at him, "And why do you even care? Come on, tell me. And don't say it's because you're my guardian. I'm not an idiot, and I felt something from you. Right?" She put her fists on her hips and faced him directly. Her voice had sounded as much like she was asking as she was telling him.

He got a little twitch by his left eye as he turned away. He bent down to begin cleaning his sword as best he could with a bit of grass. He had his back to Eva, and I glanced over to see what she would do.

Instead of yelling at him some more, as I thought she would, she walked over to me and stood shoulder to shoulder. She said, "You know, I thought he actually liked me. Not just because he was forced to be around me. He should have been glad when I left, so he didn't have to be responsible for me anymore." She said it just loud enough to make sure Cairo heard her.

I took a deep breath and let it out slowly, feeling the frustration build. Instead of answering her, I changed the subject. "So, you think these Carnites were working for Eldrick, or did they just wander into the area?"

She looked at me like I was an idiot. "Oh, come on. I know you heard them say they were going to turn me in to King Eldrick and he was giving them the Congo. Now you're just stalling. You're as bad as he is." She stomped away and sat down, leaning against a tree at the edge of the clearing.

Over by the Carnites, Cairo stood slowly, stretched his back, and then started walking east. Over his shoulder he said, "Come on. We shouldn't stay here and we have a long way to go, thanks to her." He didn't even look back.

I glanced over at Eva and shrugged. When I started following him, Eva fell in line a few feet behind me. It would've been a lot easier to just call out my dragon, but I was far too exhausted to fly. I was sure they were, too, since no one mentioned the idea. Not only was my mahier about drained, but I was physically exhausted.

We walked through the jungle in a straight line, spaced out a little bit, alone with our own thoughts. One of us occasionally stopped and grabbed something edible. With our mahier drained so much, I was sure they were starving just as much as I was. We were in kind of a desperate situation, but there was nothing we could do but keep walking. So we did.

After a few more hours, Eva finally caught up to me. Her hands were in her pockets and her eyes were on the ground, watching where she put her feet so she didn't fall. I also thought it might be her way of not having to look at anyone. I mean, even as clumsy as I was, I still managed to glance up every once in a while. That's how I knew Eva had caught up.

Quietly, I said, "How are you doing? I know you've got to be exhausted."

She nodded. "Yeah, I'm tired. And half the reason I'm so exhausted is that I'm starving."

I simply nodded. It was all true, so what could I say? We walked on in silence for a few minutes, but I noticed she kept up with me, always beside me. Maybe she had something on her mind, but I wasn't going to push.

Eventually, she said, "Actually, I do have something on my mind. I mean, besides just how hungry I am. It's Cairo. Don't you think he's been acting a little weird lately? Like, every time I come around, he stops laughing or talking. I keep catching him looking at me out of the corner of my eye."

I began to feel a little uncomfortable. I never really liked to get caught up in the middle of Eva and other people. She could be unpredictable and wild, and sometimes her frustration got pointed at me. It was the last thing I wanted to deal with, as tired as I was. She kept looking at me like she expected a response, though. "Maybe he's just keeping an eye on you, since that's his job."

"Maybe. But I think it's more than that. I thought we were getting along really well, you know? And then all of this. Now I think he was just trying to get along because it made his job easier. I don't think he really liked me at all."

I felt my heat rise and I began to sweat. Part of me wanted to tell her the truth, just to get it out in the open, and because it would make her feel better. She clearly cared what Cairo thought of her.

But before I opened my mouth, I decided it wasn't my place to say anything. I knew how he felt, but only because he told me. It was up to him to tell Eva when he wanted to. So I tried to dodge it. "What's not to like about you? Sure, you're headstrong and stubborn. And you do reckless things, mostly because you're way braver than I am. But you're also a really good person, that's why you decided to be my friend, right? You were the only person at school who took a chance to get to know me." Then I forced myself to laugh a little and said, "Then again, look how that worked out for you."

She let out a deep sigh, but we walked on in silence for quite a while. I didn't know how much later it was, but eventually, she said, "Cole, do you think I did the right thing going after the Mermaids?" She hesitated a bit and I could hear the worry in her voice. "Right now, it seems like it might have been kind of foolish."

Of course she was worried. She'd made a decision that should have been all of ours, one that could spell victory or doom for the dragons, all the other mythical creatures, and even humankind itself. "Of course you did the right thing. I mean, running off like that was stupid, but sometimes you do stupid stuff."

I turned my head to look at her and grinned. When I got a faint smile back, I continued, "But seriously. I don't think we really had any other choice, so yes, I think you did the right thing. Most of the Elves are already captured, and the rest have limited tilium until their wards are restored. We don't know where the loyalties lie for most of the other magical creatures, so going to Greece wasn't a great option."

Her face showed a bit of relief. She ran her fingers through her sweat-damp hair, pushing it back out of her face. "We don't know where the loyalties of the Mermaids are, either, though."

"All the things we've heard about them tell me they aren't rushing to join up with Eldrick. They may only be minor players up here on land with us dragons, but water covers most of the Earth. Why would they want to sign up to be Eldrick's slaves, when they're the masters of most of the planet?"

She put her hand on my back as we sat down side by side. "Thanks, Cole. I knew I could count on you for the truth, even if I didn't want to hear it. You're a good guy, you know? That's the biggest reason I decided to be your friend, way back in the day. But doesn't that seem like a whole different lifetime ago?"

I chuckled. "Yeah, it does. I think—"

Out in the jungle, off to my right, I heard a sudden loud *crack!* It rolled over us and echoed off the trees and hills like thunder, deep and rumbling. I fought down the sudden urge to run. Then I heard another crack, another rumble. This time, though, it came from somewhere to our left. Eva and I looked at each other, eyes wide with shock and fear.

Chapter Eleven

As the sounds grew louder, we took off running at the same time. Whatever was coming at us, I sure didn't want to meet it. We jumped over fallen logs, went around trees, and once, I grabbed a vine without slowing down to swing over a coiled snake. I didn't know what kind it was, and I was pretty sure my mahier would be able to handle a snake bite just fine, but it would slow me down. I felt the sweat building on the back of my neck and on my forehead, and after half a mile, I was panting.

The whole time we ran, whatever was crashing through the jungle was getting closer. We had been running a few miles when I heard the deep, frightening noise right behind me. I risked a glance over my shoulder, but what I saw surprised me. It wasn't some strange beast, and it wasn't a Carnite. It was an Elden. I saw it reach out and somehow zap a tree with its tilium. The tree was only damaged, though, not even destroyed. That was what had been making the noise.

I saw the Elden were stretched out in a row, half a dozen that I could see. They were randomly zapping trees as they ran toward us. There was no way I wanted to get hit with that, though I was curious why they were shooting trees, so I ran even faster. We had to put some distance between us and them because even if the ones I saw were all of them, we were outnumbered. I was pretty sure there were more I hadn't seen.

As I caught up to Cairo, I said, "Run faster, it's the Elden! Shooting trees... At least six of them..."

Eva and Cairo sped up. Another mile went by, and I could hear the Elden finally falling farther behind. We were getting away! I was exhausted, but I had my tilium to draw from. I knew we were all low on mahier, yet they kept up. Cairo and Eva were just in better shape than me, I guessed.

The jungle kept going on and on, but there was no way to tell how much farther it stretched. I hoped it didn't run out before we could escape and hide again, though I wasn't sure where to hide if they were zapping all the trees. I sure didn't want to get mistaken for a tree. Cairo's trick where he made their tilium senses see all the trees looking like us wouldn't work now that they were just blasting away. I wondered how they had enough tilium to keep that going.

I was in the middle of that thought when Cairo let out a yelp. I turned to look, and saw him streaking up into the air. I skidded to a stop and turned back, then realized he had stumbled into a simple, old-fashioned net trap. In the distance, the rumbling sound of the Elden's blasting continued.

Without hesitating, Eva jumped up and grabbed onto a lower branch, then scrambled up the tree like a monkey. In moments, I'd lost sight of her, but shortly after, Cairo came crashing to the ground, wrapped in the net. I helped him get out of the net, then we looked up into the tree.

From above, I heard Eva shouting, "Get up here. Hurry."

I didn't know what she had in mind, but we didn't have time to argue. Cairo and I scrambled up the trunk and found ourselves in the dense foliage.

It took a while, but two scratches on my face and one small cut on my hand later, we reached Eva.

Panting, I asked, "Why are we up here?"

Eva held up her hand to be quiet. I saw that she had her eyes closed. The seconds ticked by, then she said, "Instead of making all the trees look like us, I'm making us blend in with this tree."

"When they blast this tree, is that going to matter?" Cairo asked.

She said, almost in a whisper, "They won't shoot us up this high. When they had almost caught up to us, one of them did that thing to a tree just ahead of me, and it hit about chest-high. They're only checking to see if we've disguised ourselves as trees."

I nodded, then heard the sounds of movement below. I looked, but I couldn't see anything through the leaves. We sat silently, waiting. Cairo had his eyes closed, and his lips were moving but I couldn't hear what he was saying. And I heard the sounds of Elden everywhere below us, stretching out to either direction, way more than six of them.

After they had passed, I realized I had been holding my breath and let it out.

Cairo said, "That was way too close. Something is definitely wrong here."

"Why do you say that?" Eva asked. "I mean, we got away, right?"

"How are they following us?" He turned to look at me.

I shrugged. "I don't think they're following us. They must just know the area and they're looking as hard as they can, but they're not following us. I think."

Cairo let out a long, frustrated breath. "No way. This is twice now that they've come right at us. Once, I could see. Twice? That's deliberate. Elden are evil, but they've never followed us like this. I wish I knew what was going on."

I didn't know, either, so I didn't answer.

After enough time had passed for the Elden to be long gone, we carefully climbed down and made camp for the night.

***

Back in the land of ice and snow and the beautiful lights in the sky, I hovered over the field. Again, it felt more like a vision than a dream. Midway through it, I realized I really was dreaming, but I couldn't wake up so I just watched.

When I awoke, it wasn't the panic-filled jolt that made me sit bolt upright, the way the others had. I just opened my eyes, and knew I had to tell Eva and Cairo. They were still asleep, so I settled back into the leaves I used for bedding and slept restlessly until morning.

Once everybody was fully awake, I said, "So. I had another dream."

Cairo rolled his eyes, but Eva frowned and asked, "What was it about this time?"

"Eldrick is there in the north with the missing Elves. He's giving them each a choice—either join him and become dark Elves, or lose their tilium. Most of them are taking the deal, from what I saw. He's turning them one by one. It seemed to take a long time to turn each one into a dark Elf, but Eldrick has time."

"Thanks for calling them dark Elves," Cairo said. "Those are not Elden, whatever deal they're making. They're still my friends, Gaber's family."

I nodded. No surprise he had caught that, but it just didn't feel right calling them Elden. They weren't really Elden, they were just Elves who had gone dark. "I think the Elden are like that forever. I hope they get the chance to come back to the light, someday."

Eva put her hand on Cairo's shoulder sympathetically. "I think the longer they're dark, the harder it will be. We have to hurry. If we don't rescue them soon, Eldrick will have a new army of dark Elves behind him."

At last, Cairo blew out a harsh breath and said, "It is what it is. We need to get to the Mermaids quickly and I just hope that, when they join us, they have what we need to go rescue our friends."

I hoped so, too.

J.A. Culican

Chapter Twelve

As we soared through the clouds, I could see the shores of the Dead Sea far ahead. Thankfully, once our mahier had recharged a bit, we had all been able to summon our dragons. We kept our speed slow so we didn't need to spend mahier on keeping the air around us still, and after a bit, I had more energy.

I felt a little tingling in my mind and realized Eva was trying to talk, so I opened up my perceptions and let her in. We had spent most of the journey in silence, so I was curious. "Is everything okay?"

"Yes, I'm fine. I've just been thinking about these visions or whatever they are. You say they feel different from a normal dream, right?"

"Yes." I was interested to see where this was going. "I have lots of dreams, and nightmares even, about Eldrick, but sometimes they just feel different. I know in my gut they aren't dreams."

"I didn't really believe you before, but you keep having them. And you've never been the kind of guy to make things up. Heck, it took you longer to believe in all this dragon stuff than me."

Finally. Someone was paying attention. I'd figured if anyone would believe me, it'd be Eva, and it had hurt when she'd dismissed me. Excited, I asked, "So I take it you've been thinking about this? Got any ideas?"

"No, but I think it's important for us to figure out where these dreams are coming from. The more I think about them, the more they scare me."

That was surprising. "Even if they're visions, not just dreams, I don't see why they would scare you. They scare me, but I'm the one with the nightmares."

"But we don't know why you're having them, and I have to wonder if Eldrick is somehow using them against you. Your visions are just as likely to be coming from him as from anywhere else, right? Maybe more likely. And if he's sending them, it's not to help you. What trick does he have up his sleeve? If he's sending them, he has a sneaky plan."

That was definitely something to think about. I hadn't considered that before. But I didn't really have time to think about it at the moment—Cairo banked down and to the left, heading toward the Dead Sea shoreline. We were finally there, where the Mermaids were supposed to live.

I heard Cairo's voice in my head saying, "Look alive, Keepers. We're here, and we don't know what kind of reception we'll get."

We swept downward, flying low above the scattered trees, and landed about twenty feet from the water. I managed to land without doing a face-plant, so it was a good landing as far as I was concerned. Then we called our humans and shifted.

We wandered around the beach, slowly making our way toward the water. I wasn't really sure what to look for, but I figured if there were Mermaids around, I'd see something unusual. We searched an area about 100 feet long between the scattered tree line and the water, but none of us found anything worth mentioning.

Cairo whistled, and we all gathered together by the water. "I don't really understand. The last time I was here was maybe a century ago, but they had lines of shells and trees planted in different formations, showing us where to find them. I didn't see any of that from the air, and I'm not seeing it here on the ground. I wonder where they went."

He scratched his head, and I looked past him, out over the water, trying to imagine what a Mermaid city would look like down there. Then I noticed ripples in the water, and my eyes went wide.

Cairo spun around to see what I was looking at, then froze. At least a dozen people were rising up out of the water. I knew right away they were Mermaids, from the watery plants woven into their braided hair to the slightly blue skin. I thought I saw flaps behind the ears of one who turned to look at the others, but I couldn't be sure. I also didn't know how they would get out of the water, but then they just walked right out, legs and all. Each of them carried a short spear or trident. They were a couple inches shorter than most people, and I could see webbed fingers wrapped around their weapons. I was a little disappointed they didn't have fish tails.

The twelve of them kept their weapons pointed toward us and moved into a circle, with us in the middle. I found myself turning my back to Cairo, and saw Eva do the same, so the three of us were facing outward at the Mermaids.

One who was a deeper shade of blue than the others said, "Hold. Put down your weapons now. I warn you to do as I say." His voice had a sort of wet, bubbly sound, and came out raspy. Along with his sharp, pointy teeth and big, fin-like ears, the water plants woven into his green hair, green glowing eyes...he looked kind of creepy.

I slowly drew my sword, then tossed it into the sand a few feet away.

Cairo hissed, "What are you doing, Keeper?" I could hear the concern in his voice. He might even have been afraid.

I said, "We're here to see the Mermaids, aren't we? Well, they're not going to talk to us while we're armed. There's too many of them for us to fight off, anyway. Just do what they say, and trust in Fate."

I heard two more swords land in the sand. Thank goodness, because I hadn't been sure Cairo would do it.

The Mermaid nodded. "That was smart of you. I will ask you this once: what do dragons want with Mermaids? You wanted nothing to do with us when we needed your help, but now you come here alone. We hear things about what is going on out there, so you're either here to ask for help or to demand it. In either case, you have wasted your trip. Leave, or die."

Cairo held up both hands and took one step toward the leader. "I don't think you understand the situation. This is the Time of Fear, and these two with me are the Keeper of Dragons—the Golden Dragon and the Prince. Your queen will want to hear of this."

The dark blue Mermaid lowered his trident a little. His gaze clicked over to me and Eva, then back to Cairo. "You lie. They are too young."

Cairo shook his head. "No. They grew up within a mile of each other among the humans. You think that's a coincidence?"

"Then they grew in strength so close to each other... But that's impossible."

Cairo shrugged. "It's very possible. And it's the truth. All signs point to the Time of Fear. We've come to ask the help of the Mermaids, and I know we failed in our duty to you, once, but if the Elves and Trolls can forgive us for our foolish century, maybe Queen Desla can, too."

The Mermaid turned to the others and said something that sounded like trying to sing while gargling water. The soldiers kept their spears and tridents pointed at us and inched closer.

Their leader said, "Come. I will take you to our queen, not as guests, but as prisoners. She will decide what to do with you."

From his tone of voice, I got the impression he hoped they would just kill us and be done with it. It seemed Ochana had a lot of making up to do for whatever they had done in the past to all these different peoples. We were prodded toward the water, and I wondered if they were just going to drown us. Cairo didn't seem concerned, so I hesitantly followed him.

J.A. Culican

Chapter Thirteen

I found myself holding my breath, which made sense because I was underwater. Half a minute later, I panicked. I turned and tried to run back to shore, but it was really more like thrashing. As soon as my head broke the surface, I took deep gasps. I hadn't even worried about the Mermaids with spears.

When I turned back around, I found the Mermaids standing half out of the water, staring at me. Cairo and Eva looked amused, while our captors looked irritated. I looked at Cairo and said, "What?"

Eva rolled her eyes. "Didn't you pay attention during our training?" Eva paused and shook her head at me. "It's just like when we fly and use our mahier to keep the wind from tearing us apart. Use it to lock a bubble of air around your head, and just draw fresh oxygen from the water."

Cairo shook his head and let out a frustrated sigh, like he was dealing with toddlers. "You both need to pay more attention during training. Anytime someone with power—mahier or tilium—goes into the water with Mermaids around, you can just breathe the water. It doesn't even get into your lungs. I mean, as long as they aren't trying to kill you."

I felt my face flush. Of course my mahier would work underwater. Of course there was more to it than just Mermaids driving us to our doom. Otherwise, Cairo wouldn't have calmly walked into the Dead Sea. "Okay. I'm sorry. I've never tried to breathe underwater before, so it didn't occur to me that I could."

Cairo turned back around and walked away from shore. "Of course it didn't. Stop fooling around, and let's go."

We headed back into the water, and although I paused just before my head went under, I took a deep breath and felt my mahier around me. I trusted that way more than I trusted the Mermaids to keep me alive down there.

My wet clothes stuck to me as we walked for what seemed like a mile, and at first it was really slow going. Then Cairo was in my head, telling me to just use my mahier to open the way, just as we did with the air when we were flying fast. After that, it got a lot easier. I was kind of tired of feeling dumb, and all of that would have been good to know before I embarrassed myself in front of the Mermaids.

All around us were Mermaids swimming faster than I could run on dry land. Only our captors seemed to bother walking, and I got the impression they were only doing it for us. The Mermaid town had no walls, just like all the other fantastical creatures' homes I had been to. They must have had wards, though I didn't feel any of it. Cairo explained that their tilium was different from the Elves'.

Once we got to the town proper, my eyes bulged. It was one of the most beautiful things I had ever seen. Every dwelling, every building, had been made to look like seashells or choral, or had been woven out of the many plants that grew all over. I hadn't seen any such plants before we got to the town, so they were probably hidden from outsiders.

The light was murky down here, but there were hundreds or even thousands of small, floating globes tethered in place, shining brightly. They gave off enough light to see by. I had noticed our guards' eyes were a lot larger than a human's or Elf's, and then I knew why. It was so they could see better in the dim light at the bottom of the Dead Sea.

There were no streets, so we did end up having to swim. After a little bit of practice, Cairo taught me how to use my mahier not just to keep myself breathing, but to sort of push myself through the water, almost like swimming. No, more like flying. That would've been a lot more exciting before I had flown halfway around the world as a dragon, but it was still kind of cool.

We got to what I assumed was the palace. It was the biggest building in the Mermaid town, and the only one that didn't blend perfectly with the nature all around. It was obviously constructed, a large dome with towers all over it.

We were led into the castle through a huge arch that spanned twenty feet or more. Inside, it was even more beautiful. There were marble tiles on the floor, marble walls, marble pillars holding the dome up. I wondered whether the pillars were decorative, though, because I thought domes didn't need support.

It didn't seem like the right time to ask about the architecture, though, so the three of us meekly followed our guards across the gorgeous foyer, then down a long hall lined with guards standing at attention. We reached a huge set of double doors, and the guards posted there opened them for us.

I looked inside and saw what must have been the biggest room in the castle. A dome inside a dome, it was a couple hundred feet across, and I couldn't really tell how high the ceiling was at its peak. There were so many of the glowing balls embedded into the walls that it was almost as bright as daylight. It was a softer glow, though, and didn't hurt my eyes. With the Mermaids' huge eyes, I was surprised it didn't hurt theirs, but they didn't seem to flinch.

We were marched up to a lone woman sitting on a raised throne. She stared ahead, looking bored, ignoring the dozens of Mermaids wandering around the throne room below her, talking in little groups.

When we got closer, a dozen more armed Mermaids appeared out of person-sized archways to either side of the platform and formed a semi-circle around their queen.

I almost didn't notice her because I was so busy looking at the crowd of Mermaids. Down in their own homeland, they didn't bother with legs. Just like the old drawings, they had tails, but no scales. More like a dolphin's tail.

When we got to the platform, one of our captors said, "Kneel before Queen Desla and pay your respects. Pray she is merciful, all hail the queen."

I didn't need to be told twice. I knelt right away, as did Cairo. Eva was slower, but followed us down. The room grew quiet, all the hushed conversations stopping at once, and all eyes turned to us. It was pretty intimidating, but there was no backing out.

She said, "What is the meaning of this. Why do dragons invade my realm? Answer true, or die."

That wasn't the warm welcome I had hoped for. Cairo glanced at me and tilted his head toward the queen. He wanted me to talk? I supposed it was up to me as the Keeper of Dragons.

"Hail, Queen Desla of the Mermaids. I'm Cole, the Keeper, and this is Eva, the Golden Dragon. We beg an audience with the queen." I held my breath and prayed what I said was right.

Her eyes shifted to Cairo, who only nodded very slightly, and then her eyes were back on me. "I asked a question, dragon."

My mind raced. What question? Then I remembered. "I'm sorry, but we haven't come to invade. We've come in peace, and to warn you."

Several of the guards took an angry step toward me, lowering their pitchforks and spears at me, but the queen said quietly, "Hold."

The guards stepped back into place, but eyed me angrily.

Hastily, I said, "Not to warn you about us! I mean to let you know of danger. As friends."

Desla tilted her head back and laughed. It was a sweet, musical sound. Her eyes showed no joy, though. "I have no need of protection from you, or from any dragon. Why are you here, and what is your warning? Speak quickly."

I spent the next twenty minutes telling her my story, even the parts I wasn't really proud of. She had to know the whole story to know I was telling the truth about the Time of Fear arriving. I ended by telling her that the Keeper of Dragons was fated to end the Time of Fear, but that it was time for the Mermaids to play their part, a very important part.

She was quiet for a long moment. She stared at me, unblinking—actually, I had not seen any of them blink—and found myself holding my breath. I had to consciously make myself take even breaths, and my heart was racing.

At last, she said, "Colton, Prince of Ochana, I have heard your story, and I am unmoved. We are safe here in the water, as we always have been. A few hundred years ago, I might have joined you, but we do not forget that the dragons turned a blind eye to the fighting and suffering of the Elves, Trolls, and others of our kind. We took in many refugees during that time, and lent our soldiers to the Elves. Meanwhile, you hid in your clouds and did nothing."

This wasn't going according to plan. I felt the opportunity slipping away. I had to say something! "My Queen, I don't think you—"

"Silence!" Her shout echoed across the room, and I saw even a couple of soldiers flinch. She must not raise her voice very often, but then again, why would a queen need to? I lowered my eyes so I wasn't looking at her directly and shut my mouth.

"I have no wish to harm dragons. Our friendship goes back almost to the beginning, and you've done us no wrong, personally. If the Elves and Trolls and Fairies can forgive you, who am I to hold that grudge for them? So, go in peace, Keeper of Dragons. I wish you well, but you will have no Mere help. Maybe if you had come sooner, we could have helped, but the damage is done. The Elves and Trolls are gone, the Fairies divided. The dragons fight alone, now. Be gone from my kingdom."

I stood there with my mouth open, stunned. We had come all this way, faced all those dangers, risked our lives... And now the Mermaids would do nothing? We had come here for nothing, when we could have been searching the north to look for the imprisoned Elves and Trolls. Like a light switch, my shock and disbelief turned to anger, burning the common sense right out of my head.

I glowered at their queen. "How dare you call the Elves your friends? You don't care about the Trolls, the Fairies. You sit here safe in your lake while your so-called friends suffer."

"How dare you—"

"They're dying out there! And the Elves probably wish they were dying. Do you know what King Eldrick is doing to them? He's forcing the Elves to choose between losing their magic or becoming dark Elves. Slaves. You want to talk about the dragons sitting by and doing nothing? At least we're out there fighting, and don't think for one minute that when Eldrick is done with the dragons he won't turn on you, too. You sit here safe and sound until the end, and then there won't be anyone left to help you when it's your turn!"

I think the only reason I was able to say all that before one of their guards knocked me to the ground was that it was such a surprise. They didn't expect it. But then one did slam me down and stood over me with his trident, ready to plunge it right into my heart. I only survived because the queen shouted, "Hold! Do not harm the young dragon."

Every eye in the throne room flicked from me to the queen. They all looked surprised, probably because she had let me talk to her like that without killing me on the spot. I wondered if she had even worse in store for me than just death, but I didn't care. I sat straight up, my fists clenched, staring her in the eyes, daring her to tell me I was wrong.

For the first time, she rose from her throne. She glided to me and stopped ten feet away, then floated there, looking me in the eyes. The way my heart was beating, every second seemed like a minute. I waited for my fate, too angry at her to care what she did next. If she didn't help, we were all dead, anyway.

She lowered her eyes and bent at the waist in a half-bow, then said, "Keeper, your words ring true, and they shame me. They shame us all. It is hard to imagine that a dragon so young spoke more truth than the Mermaids."

I climbed back to my feet and looked at her suspiciously. I didn't know where it was going, but at least she hadn't yet ordered them to do something horrible to me or my friends. "My apologies for my outburst, Queen Desla. As a guest here, I shouldn't talk to you like that, but what you said made me so mad I just didn't know what to do with myself."

She nodded slowly, considering. Then she said, "The war is coming here sooner or later. If it comes sooner, we have allies, allies who won't be there if it comes later. The only hope for all the Elves, Trolls, Fairies and eventually the dragons, is for the Mermaids to stand up now and do what is right."

"Yes! Stand up for the Truth, while you still can. I'm begging you, help us save them all. And yourselves." I glanced over at Cairo and Eva and saw them staring at me incredulously. I'd surprised them just as much as I had the Queen.

Desla said, "I accept your apology, Colton, Keeper of Dragons. I feel the truth in your words and the goodness in your heart. Your anger wasn't misplaced."

My heart leaped and my anger vanished. Excited, I blurted, "So you'll help us? You'll march with us against the Elden?"

The Queen smiled, but I thought it looked sad, not happy. "This still isn't our war. We always kept to ourselves, only helping the Elves and the others during the last war because you dragons neglected your duties. As I said, if the Elves can forgive you, surely I can."

She let out a long breath, her bubbles rising up and out of sight toward the ceiling. "Alas, the Mermaids will not march with you. However, I feel obligated to help our other brethren."

I wasn't sure what to think of that. "What help will you give, then? We're grateful for any help."

"Instead of sending soldiers, I will send you wisdom and knowledge. I will help you by training you and your two friends here, showing you how to defeat Eldrick and this new threat. With the knowledge we will give you, I'm confident you will win in the end. If you truly are the Keeper of Dragons, then Fate will make sure that truth wins. Eldrick and his lies will fall. This is the best we can do."

I was disappointed. "The best you *will* do, you mean."

For the first time, I saw Queen Desla's genuine smile, and it lit up her face. I didn't know what I had said that was so amusing. "That's right. It's the most that we *will* do. If the legends are wrong and the

Fates do not intend for you to win in the end, then we must look after ourselves as we always have. I feel you were brought here for a reason, and I think that reason is to seek the wisdom and knowledge to stand up to Eldrick yourselves, as the legends say you must."

From what little I heard of the legends, she had a point. I was still disappointed about the troops, though. But at least we weren't thrown out or worse. Something told me the Mermaids didn't allow outsiders in often, if at all.

I guessed I would take what I could.

Chapter Fourteen

I was pretty sure that if we hadn't been in the middle of the Dead Sea, I would have been sweating a whole lot after the workout they gave us. The Mermaid who put us through our paces said they only meant to get a feel for our physical condition. I guess that swimming everywhere his whole life gave him the kind of endurance and strength matched only by athletes.

All I knew was that I was dog-tired after only an hour of swimming hard. I looked at him and said, "How did we do?"

Cairo and Eva turned their heads to our conversation, probably trying to hear his answer.

"You are Ochana's warriors, yet your stamina is like a Mere child's. Humans and dragons must not train the way we do." He smirked, but I sensed that he was just giving us a good-natured ribbing.

After the session, we were led back to the quarters they'd given us. It was a fairly large dome with entrances on both sides which angled down into the Dead Sea floor before coming back up again. The water had been pumped out, replaced with air, and it was actually pretty dry once we got inside. I glanced at my hands; I'd never seen them so wrinkly. I wondered if they might start rotting off with enough time in the water.

We sat at the one table in the place, which had four chairs around it. I propped my elbows on the table and rested my face in my hands.

Cairo said, "Tired, are you? I can't blame you. All I want to do is sleep."

"Me, too," Eva chimed in. She sounded as tired as I felt.

Cairo sat and rested his chin on one fist and drummed his fingers loudly on the table.

"Something on your mind?" I asked. "You look like something is bugging you."

He stared at the table, and I could almost see the gears turning in his mind. "I'm just uneasy. We're here among the Mermaids like Eva wanted, but they don't want to help us. We're basically at their mercy, right? I mean, we're underwater. Their environment. Their homeland. What if they decide to take the easy way out and try to buy Eldrick's goodwill by turning us over? I don't know that we can trust these Mermaids. Their reaction when we showed up was definitely not what I expected."

Eva let out a long breath and rolled her eyes. "I understand how you feel, but really, if we're fated to win the war and push back the Time of Fear, then everything will turn out okay. We're stuck here for now and we need them. So, I suggest we do what they say and just go off the assumption they won't backstab us. What choice do we have but to trust them?"

Cairo shook his head, looking unconvinced. "Yes, but if they betray us, we're in the middle of the Dead Sea. There's literally nowhere to go. We could never make it to the surface before they caught up to us."

I thought Cairo was being dangerously paranoid, so I interrupted him before he got on a roll and convinced himself to do something stupid. "The Mermaids haven't given us any reason to mistrust them. They've made it clear they don't want to help us, but here they are, helping us anyway. And you're right, there's nothing we could do if they decided to betray us. So, no offense, but I think that as long as we're stuck here, it might be best not to make your fears be a self-fulfilling prophecy."

Eva nodded. "Cole's right. The more you treat people like enemies, the more they will be, right? That's how it worked in high school, and it seems to be how it works out here in the so-called real world, too."

He grinned. "So-called? What do you mean by that?"

"I'm still not convinced this isn't just all a bad dream." She reached out and knocked his elbow out from under him, and his head almost hit the table as she laughed.

I left them talking and play-fighting and went to bed. I could barely keep my eyes open after the day's workouts.

***

The next morning, we woke, dressed, and ate the meager breakfast someone had left on the table for us. As I returned the dishes to the counter, a splashing noise drew our attention to the entrance.

A Mermaid with a spear walked up the ramp from the air hatch. Once he could see all three of us, he said, "Your presence is requested at the training grounds. Today's training will be different, so I hope you all got rest." I wanted to ask questions, but he turned around and left without another word.

I turned to Eva and Cairo. "Yesterday's training was terrible, but I already feel stronger. No wonder the Mermaids are supposed to be the strongest of us all."

Eva said, "Yeah, they spend all day swimming, every day of their lives. It's like wearing weights around your wrists and ankles all the time. I guess we should get going."

We walked to the murky water at the bottom of the air tunnel, then swam through the town to reach the training grounds. At the field's far end, a small cluster of Mermaids gathered, but I couldn't make out any faces. I figured those were our trainers for the day, so I veered a little to the right, aiming toward them. When we were about twenty feet away, I let myself drift to the bottom, then continued on foot. The small crowd of half a dozen stepped aside, revealing Queen Desla herself. She didn't smile, but she did nod in greeting, so I did the same.

"Keeper of Dragons, I hear your training yesterday went well," she said. "Today, I will be your instructor. While I work with each Keeper individually to show you the ways of our mereum magic, the other two will work with my hand-picked team of instructors to master our style of war. History has shown that not even the dragons can defeat us, unless we were greatly outnumbered. Ours is a defensive style that focuses on allowing our opponents to tire themselves while we wait for the opportunity to strike. That is when the fight usually ends."

I was in total awe. "Mermaids have fought dragons before?"

She grinned and held her chin up as she said, "No, of course not. We're all on the side of truth. But there have been... What do you call them on the surface? 'Joint training maneuvers.' That's it. Long ago, we all used to train together—dragons, Elves, Trolls, and many of the other good-hearted creatures of the world."

I hadn't been told that, but it made sense since the current war was supposed to be the closest the True beings had come to being defeated. And the fact that we all had stopped training together also made sense after the dragons had our time of being completely self-absorbed. In a way, I was kind of honored to be the first dragon to train with Mermaids in a long time, and I gave Desla a polite bow.

She said, "Cole, will you please follow me? We will get out of everyone's way to practice our water magic. I will instruct you personally. Cairo, Eva, will you please go with my instructors? *Your* training begins today, as well."

Cairo bowed. Grinning back at her, he said, "I thought yesterday was when our training started."

"If only that were true," she said, eyes twinkling, "but that was only the warm-up."

The other Mermaids dragged my friends away and I followed Desla onto the sidelines. I thought the training arena looked a lot like a football stadium. When she took my hands in hers, I could feel a kind of energy flowing through everything around us. I hadn't noticed it the day before. I sensed an energy flowing between our touching hands, too. It wasn't mahier, but it also wasn't tilium.

Maybe she read my mind or maybe it was a lucky guess, but she said, "That's right, the Mermaids have a kind of power all our own. It comes from the waters all around us. Even when we walk among you air-breathers on dry land, water is still all around us in every plant, every animal, even in the air itself."

I was impressed. "You draw power even from humidity in the air!"

She shrugged. "More like the water is a channel that lets us use and manipulate our mereum. But that power also gives us control of water itself, the element of Life. We can gather it or scatter it, move it and make it do as we wish. Down here, where everything is water, we are at our most powerful. It is also the hardest to see our power in action down here for the same reason. Just as you can't see the wind within the air, you cannot see mereum at work when you are surrounded by water."

I was astounded. She definitely had my attention. "Even the water in the air we breathe? What can you make it do?"

"Anything you can imagine, once you have practiced a particular spell. For example, I can create tendrils made of water that obey my commands. I could use them to bind you, or I could have them strangle you. I can make the water gather inside someone's lungs, or I can move water out of their brain. Those kinds of deadly attacks require months of training, even years. Not even every Mermaid reaches that level of mastery. But I will teach you what little you can learn in the short time we have together. It will be one more weapon in your arsenal."

I bowed again. I was surprised that Queen Desla, who hadn't even wanted us here, was willing to try to teach me to use the power of the Mermaids. The only explanation I could think of was that she at last believed I was the Keeper of Dragons, and that the Time of Fear really was at hand.

For the next hour, she taught me the Mere water magic, mereum. The thing we practiced the longest was simply how to reach out with my senses and feel the water through my power. She said I couldn't begin to control the water until I could sense it with my mereum. I wasn't sure I had any, but I went along with it.

At one point, I glanced toward Eva and Cairo where they were desperately trying to learn how to fight with the Mere spears and weird, small shields. Their opponents continually got around their shields, delivering what would be killing blows had they been really fighting.

Desla frowned. "Pay attention, young prince. Only once you can recognize the energy that flows through the water will you begin to control it."

I eventually got to the point where I could sense the water, but only barely. After an hour, I was still a long way from learning to control it, and I was getting frustrated. When the bell rang to mark the end of the session, I was relieved. I needed to do something less frustrating for a bit.

Another hour went by with Cairo and me training with the fighting instructors, and Eva with Desla. It only took a minute or two to realize how difficult their combat style was. I did a little better than Cairo for some reason, but not by much, and my instructor seemed to take a lot of pleasure in making fun of how I was doing. He also told me that in only twenty minutes, Eva had done better than I was doing after an hour. I glanced over to where she was training with the queen. She stood with her arms stretched wide, gliding her hands back and forth through the water. I figured she was feeling the energy Desla had told me about, which was a little frustrating. That meant she was already doing better than me with mereum, too.

After we took a short break, Desla asked me to work with her again. It took a couple more hours before I was able to feel the water all around me like Eva had done hours ago. Frustrated, I wondered why I was even along for the ride.

At last, when I stretched out my hands, I felt tingling all up and down my arms, my legs, my whole body. I realized with a shock that I was finally gathering mereum. Desla said that the more I practiced, the faster I could draw it in. I'd be able to soak up mereum just from the dew on blades of grass, or even from the humidity in the air. The drier the air was, the longer it would take to pull in enough energy to use, but no air on Earth was completely dry—I could always gather mereum no matter where I was.

The drawback to mereum was that I couldn't actually hold on to that energy for long. I had to draw it in as I used it, unlike mahier. Recharging mahier quickly only happened if I ate a cow. There wouldn't always be a lucky cow around to scarf up, as I had already learned.

The next task she had me working on was to separate the water to form a ball of emptiness. It was hard because the water pressure kept smashing through my ball. At first I could only make one as big as a marble.

During a quick break while I gathered more mereum, I asked, "Can this do anything besides control the shape of water? With mahier, we can use it to push our senses outward, sometimes a great distance. There are other things we can do with it, too."

"Yes, of course. We can push our senses out, too. There is water vapor in the air, and every moving thing disturbs that vapor. Living things also are mostly made of water, and because you can sense it, no illusion can fool you if you are looking hard enough."

I grinned at her. "That would have been handy a few times already, you know."

She nodded and said, "You will also be able to cause rain, move it away from you so you stay dry, or even keep it from raining. I told you earlier that you can use mereum to flood an enemy's lungs, or dry out their organs."

I thought about how I could use this new power, so different from mahier and tilium. "So yes, I'll be able to do a lot more than just feel the water. I'm impressed, again."

"It has been a millennium since we taught anyone but our own kind how to use mereum." She grinned and added, "Your slow progress reminds me why."

I could tell it was only friendly teasing, but I still had to remind myself not to get too proud. I smiled back and focused on my training.

With more practice, my control grew better, and she began to push me harder, taking me through a series of exhausting mental exercises. Controlling mahier was all about willpower, but mereum was more about a way of thinking, of concentrating hard. I was exhausted mentally, but she said time was of the essence and I had to learn fast. That was true—we didn't have years to train like the Mermaids did. We had to leave soon. So, with her hammering away at me, I pushed myself harder and harder.

Evening was beginning to settle in when I began to tremble. My hands shook and my left eye twitched. Still, I pushed myself even harder. I was beyond exhausted and the shaking grew worse, but I didn't say anything to the queen. I pushed on and pushed harder.

Maybe an hour later, I realized I should have said something to Desla about my shaking, but it was suddenly too late. A giant tremor started at my toes and shot up my legs, along the length of my spine, and when it got to my head, my eyes rolled back and everything went black. I knew what would come next.

J.A. Culican

Chapter Fifteen

... Confusing visions ... Trolls staked out under the sun, under night skies ... in snow, in jungle, in desert, in farmlands ... I stand over them, one after the other and all at once ... I hold a knife I've never seen before ... I say words I don't understand ... the knife plunges into a Troll's heart ... the snow melts, the desert scrubland turns sandy, the jungle withers, the crops die ...

... I rise up above the scene of another Troll ... I see King Eldrick, laughing, holding the knife ... the Troll dies, the land dies ...

My eyes flew open as I sat bolt upright. I was confused about where I was, then realized I was still underwater, still in the Mermaid city, still in the training yard. Only now, a crowd of Mermaids had joined my companions to stand around me as Eva and Cairo knelt beside me. Eva had my head in her lap, and she looked worried. But the Mermaids didn't look worried for me. Their faces were painted with shock as they all stared at me. Many had mouths open, jaws dropped. Queen Desla looked pale and her eyes were wide and fearful.

What had I done to shock everyone during my vision?

As I tried to figure out how to tell the queen what I'd seen, someone in the crowd shouted, "Banish him!" I could hear the fear in his voice. A woman repeated it, and then more Mermaids took up the call. In seconds, the crowd was chanting it, their tone getting louder and angrier each time they said it.

Queen Desla stared at me. Her face was set in stone, her lips pursed tightly. I wished I could tell what she was thinking, but it sure didn't look good for me.

Eva helped me sit and had to shout in my ear for me to hear her say, "It was different this time. It was like a seizure. Your whole body shook, and we couldn't get it to stop, even with the queen's magic helping."

Desla turned to face the crowd and raised her hands into the air, fingers spread apart, and the riot of shouts died down to an angry murmur. In a strong, clear voice, she said, "The dragon is not possessed, and you are safe from harm. We will not exile them, but they will not be here much longer. Now go! Return to your homes and leave me to do my duty."

The murmuring started again, but the Mermaids did as she commanded. In a minute, we were alone and I breathed a sigh of relief. If that mob had attacked us, there was no way we could have stopped it.

She said, "Come with me, Keeper. I have something to discuss with you, but not here."

I got to my feet, a little shaky still. Cairo and Eva tried to follow me as I stepped after the queen, but I told them not to worry about me. They didn't look happy about it, but for once, they didn't argue.

I followed Desla out of the training area, through a bit of the town, and then down a narrow, winding path through a field of plants that looked like kelp.

They grew about twice my height, and it felt a bit confining.

After a few minutes, the path opened up into a small clearing about twenty feet across. A large, flat rock in the middle was big enough for us both to sit on, so we did, side-by-side. My curiosity was killing me. "Thanks again for breaking up the crowd. I know they were just scared. I am, too, if I'm honest."

As she looked at me, she took a deep breath and let it out slowly, air bubbles rising up and out of sight toward the surface. I felt like she was examining me. Maybe she was less sure about me being safe to be near than she told the crowd. Still, I didn't think she'd be here with me otherwise.

"What are you looking at?" I asked, grinning awkwardly.

She didn't grin back. "Cole, I'm afraid I have bad news. I had hoped this beautiful place might take some of the sting out of what I have to tell you."

My heart beat faster when she said that. "It is pretty here," I said, though I didn't really think so. I was just being polite. "So, what did you want to tell me?"

She said, "I will be blunt, since you seem to prefer that. The truth is, your visions aren't just dreams or hallucinations. I think you knew that already, in your heart. What you don't know is that you're having these visions because Eldrick is sending them to you. Each time the visions touch you, he can sense exactly where you are. That's why the Carnites and Elden kept finding you—it wasn't just a coincidence."

"That does explain a lot. How do I get rid of that? We can't finish our mission with him chasing after us all the time."

She looked away, out into the fields of seaweed she thought were so pretty, and then said, "The reason you see him and what he is doing is because when he touches your mind, you also touch his. You're seeing his memories."

"So that's why I saw him turning the Elves dark, and killing the Trolls."

Her head whipped back to me. "He's killing the Trolls? Where?"

I frowned. It was disturbing, sure, but she looked almost panicked. "All over, from what I could see.

And when he killed the Trolls, he was saying something I couldn't understand. Then the—"

She cut me off, saying, "The ground around him changed, too. Dying. Right?"

I nodded. If the visions were *real*, and the Trolls really were being killed all over the world, we were in trouble.

Almost as though she read my mind, she said, "He's poisoning the earth with a ritual, but it is one he shouldn't even know. One of his new dark Elves must have told him about it. He can only be trying to make a new Earth, one more to his benefit. That's bad for us all."

"That's an understatement. We have to stop them," I said, wishing I could make her understand the urgency I had felt since seeing the vision.

She pursed her lips and looked away. Softly, she said, "Yes, he must be stopped. There is a problem, however. These visions you are having drain your magic. But they also harm you. That's why the side effects keep getting worse, and if you have another vision... I am so sorry to tell you, it will probably kill you. I've seen this spell before, long ago."

I sat dumbfounded, staring at her. I think my jaw dropped, I was in such shock.

She paused, then added, "There is one thing that might save you, though."

She had my attention! "What? You have to tell me," I blurted.

"If you can learn to block the visions, they can't harm you anymore. We Mermaids can teach you how. It's difficult, but if you give it everything you've got, and you can dedicate your whole self to it, I can teach you to block it. The question is, can you learn it? Not many people can dedicate their entire self. Heart, mind, and spirit must be in line."

My heart sank. If I didn't master it, I would die, but my track record so far hadn't been very good. I struggled to learn the basics, so how could I learn something so powerful, so complex? In my heart, I felt like I was dead already. It was just a matter of time.

J.A. Culican

Chapter Sixteen

My two companions and I plopped down at the queen's long table in the great hall. The only other person there was the queen herself. I sat with my face in my hands, elbows on the table. I was still in shock.

Next to me, Eva had her hand on my shoulder. "It's not the end, Cole. The queen can teach you. You just have to try, with everything you've got. Please don't give up. If you do, then we all might as well give up right now."

I knew better than anyone how hard it was for me to learn even basic spells like summoning my dragon. What kind of a dragon can't summon himself? Well, I hadn't been able to, not at first. "I'm willing to try," I said, but even I could hear the defeat in my voice.

The queen slammed her hand on the table. The sharp crack echoed through the room and made me jump. She half-shouted, "Keeper of Dragons, you disappoint me. I don't care if you give up on yourself, but how can you give up on Eva? How can you give up on the dragons? What about your allies, the Elves, Trolls, Fairies... And now, the Mermaids?"

I looked up, surprised. After the way her people reacted to my latest vision, I thought she'd be kicking us out sooner rather than later. "You'll agree to a Mere Treaty?"

"Yes," she said as she sank back into her chair. "Listen. Now that Eldrick knows you're here with us, you're going to have to leave soon. I'm sorry to have to dump more bad news on you right now, but it's just the truth. But before you go, I will teach you how to resist your visions. Without you, everything is lost."

"I don't think I can do it, though. I'm going to let you down. I'll let everyone down." I'm not sure I had ever felt this helpless before.

Desla nodded slowly, taking in my words, and then she seemed to come to some sort of decision. "I am convinced you can learn this. I know you don't have much faith in yourself, but the truth is that you should have been dead after the first vision. The fact that it has taken you this long to be in real danger tells me that you have strength in you greater than almost any I have ever seen. And that makes sense, because you're the Keeper of Dragons. Fate wouldn't have put this in your hands if you couldn't handle it. Will you at least try? Let me rephrase that—you *will* try."

That was interesting news. I had never really thought of myself as being that strong, but if the queen had faith I could learn the Mere magic and protect myself, she would know better than anyone on Earth. I nodded, still not enthusiastic about our chances, but at least I had begun to feel a glimmer of hope. Maybe sometimes hope was all it took.

"Yes, I'll do it." As I looked around the room, everyone smiled with relief. They were relying on me. I decided right then and there that I wouldn't let them down.

Desla said, "Then we begin immediately, because we don't know how much time we have."

I had a sinking feeling that our time would run out before I did what needed doing.

***

For the hundredth time, I felt the Mere water energy building within me as I gathered it like she'd taught me. But yet again, when I tried to create a shield that would keep Eldrick out, it all just fizzled and the power drained away.

I had to start all over again, drawing the energy out of the water as I got ready to try the shield another time. And failed. Each time I tried, I got a little closer, but I knew I had a long way to go. Since I had no way of knowing when Eldrick would try again, the only way I would survive was to master that shield well enough to keep it up all the time, even when I was asleep. I tried to have confidence that I could do it. I told myself Fate wouldn't let me die in such a stupid way. I wasn't sure I'd win, but I just didn't want to believe I'd lose just like that.

As the energy flowed into me, I could feel it gathering in a ball in my chest. It was like a little pressure that wanted to get out. It wanted me to use it. I didn't know how I knew that, but I could tell. Or maybe it was in my imagination. Once the energy was large enough, I imagined invisible hands molding it like clay, stretching it out into a thinner and thinner layer, like rolling out bread dough.

Desla hissed in my ear, blowing my concentration. I felt the energy flow right out of me, back into the water. She said, "We're out of time. The Elden are at the Dead Sea borders. They've come for you. We can hold them off, but not forever. You have to leave now, while you still have time."

I stared at her, confused. "But I'm not ready yet. I haven't figured out the shield."

Desla had a sad look in her eyes. "It doesn't matter if you're ready yet. If you're here when the Elden arrive, they'll kill you as surely as another vision would."

After that, everything was a mad blur, like watching a movie in fast-forward. Everyone ran around, doing whatever it was Mermaids did when they were invaded. Cairo and Eva were just as frantic, gathering all their gear. I got mine ready, too, but I was just going through the motions. I felt like I was already dead, just waiting for my body to figure that out.

And then it was time to go, time to run. Yet again. I was tired of running, but it was better than dying, I supposed. I double-checked to make sure Jericho's sword was strapped tightly to my back, then we walked out together and closed another chapter of our lives.

Almost. Before we could leave, Queen Desla found us and waved us over. We met in the middle, and when she got close, she gave us some good news. "Dragons, you've done well here, and you've shown us things are as they used to be. Prince Colton here has convinced me that the dragons are again noble. When you find Eldrick and the Elves, summon us and the Mermaids will join you on the battlefield. First, though, you have to find his hiding place."

Before I could say anything, she began waving her hands in front of her in an odd pattern I hadn't seen before, more like a dance than a pattern. Her fingertips began to glow, and then it spread to her hands, then her arms. The light left a trail that didn't fade, and the more she waved her arms, the more intricate the light pattern grew.

It went out all at once, and Desla smiled at us. "I have now formally announced the Mere Treaty is in place. Prince Colton bears witness to this."

I nodded, though I didn't think it was very likely that I would live long enough to summon them. At least the dragons wouldn't die alone, though.

Desla had one more surprise for me. She grabbed my arm and dragged me to the side. I looked at her with one eyebrow raised, curious.

"I have one more thing for you before you leave. I see the sword you carry, and I recognize it as Jericho's. It is a fine sword, made by the very best weapon smiths. And yet, it's only a sword. I imagine you didn't have time to finish your training before all this began, either, and that's why you carry such a weapon. It is not good enough for the Prince of Ochana."

She had my attention. "What do you mean?"

She pinched her fingertips together on both hands, put them together, then slowly drew them apart and extended her arms. A soft, sparkling glow formed between her fingertips. It was beautiful. It looked like a million stars inside a million more, and I was mesmerized.

When she opened her fingertips, the glow stayed hovering in the water between us. She reached out and grabbed one end. The glow faded, revealing the most beautiful sword I'd ever seen. If I looked at it hard enough, I could almost see the millions and millions of stars inside it, or maybe they were just sparkles of magic. I couldn't tell, but I knew that was no normal sword.

Desla said, "Cole, this is a sword worthy of a prince or a king. It is the Mere Blade, and it has been in my family since the very first days. I would be honored if you would agree to carry this on your journey. It will be proof of the Mermaids' dedication to your cause. It's no normal sword, as I think you can tell."

I nodded, dumbstruck.

She continued, "The sword is the spirit of my people. With it, you can do amazing things. It has a mind of its own, but when the time is right—if you're ready and your heart is pure—it will know what to do. Until then, I have yet to find anything this blade won't cut through, and you can use it to channel your mahier, your tilium, and even your mereum once you learn to control it."

She held the sword out to me, and I bowed before I took it. As soon as I picked it up, I felt some sort of connection between us. It was as though her sword had bonded to me, and I knew it was deciding whether I was worthy to hold it.

After staring at the sword for a couple seconds, Desla nodded and smiled. "I knew it. Very well. Now it is time for you leave. The Elden and dark Elves are only a few miles from here. Take the sword and your companions, and run hard. Don't let them catch you, and do not rest until you master the shield I taught you."

Eva and Cairo came up beside us, and he let out a low whistle when he saw the blade. "I recognize this sword," he said with awe.

"Thank you, Queen Desla," I said. "All the members of the Mere Treaty will remember the help you gave me. If I survive, I'll bring it back to you."

"Oh, Cole, you don't need to worry about that. When it is time for the blade to come back, it will. But I do hope to see you again after you deliver us all from the Time of Fear. I wish you well. One more thing." She pulled a small, velvet bag out of her pocket and handed it to me. "I do believe you will need this as well. Just a pinch, and your guardian Jericho shall regain his strength." Without another word, she spun around and swam away, streaking through the water like a bullet. She had her own preparations to make.

I turned to Cairo and Eva and said, "It's time for us to leave. Cairo, I'd be honored if you would carry Jericho's sword for me."

I drew Jericho's sword from its sheath and gave it to him. He took it from me with a nod and slid it through his back straps. It was good to see him armed again. Then I slid the Mere Blade into my own sheath, and we left the Mermaids. I hoped it wasn't the last time I would see them.

Chapter Seventeen

A couple hours later, we had gone pretty far from the Mermaid city. I said, "We're going to Alaska. We've done what you all wanted and it turned out to be a good idea. Now it's time to do what I say. King Eldrick is somewhere in the north, halfway around the world. I don't know about you, but I'm tired of running. With or without you, I'm done putting it off. I'm going north."

Eva slid her arm through mine, and it was all she needed to say. Cairo, on the other hand, didn't say anything. He just followed us. I had expected a little more argument from him, but I guess he didn't know what else to do.

As we walked, I kept trying the Mere magic. I felt like I got better at the shield little by little, but I was still a long way from mastering it. I doubted I could do it before King Eldrick ended up killing me, which was a depressing thought.

When I was sure we were far enough away that the Elden wouldn't spot us, we summoned our dragons. We flew up through the water, using our mahier to let us move just as we did through air, until we burst out into the sky.

After a couple of hours, we were flying over some huge desert. I wasn't sure which one, since I wasn't very good at geography, but I knew Alaska was east. It was easy enough to fly east, after all, so we weren't lost.

When we were hungry, we landed and raided livestock around different oases. The houses looked different in that region, with lots of bright colors. They were built differently than anything I'd seen before, too. The cows were small and thin, which I supposed made it easier to keep them alive in that desert scrubland, but it meant we each scarfed two cows. I felt bad taking it from the farmer without asking, but he'd lose all his cows anyway if Eldrick won the war.

Then we were flying high above the earth again at blinding speeds.

I felt a tickle in my mind just before Eva's voice reached out to me. She said, "You seem quiet. What's on your mind?"

I didn't feel like lying, so I just told her the truth. "Dying. I haven't mastered the shield, and the next time Eldrick connects to find us, I imagine that'll be the end of it."

"You don't give yourself enough credit, Cole. I've seen you do amazing things. Things you thought you couldn't do. Fate has it all planned out. You just need to follow your gut and your heart, and it'll all turn out all right in the end. We'll beat the Time of Fear and push it back, and you're going to save the world. You just need to have faith in yourself. I do."

I was pretty sure she was wrong, but I didn't feel like arguing. I didn't want my last time alive to be spent bickering with my best friend, so I simply grunted.

"Cole, don't give me that. I know you. You need to listen to me, okay? Everything's going to be fine in the end. You can make the shield. Maybe not right now, but you will when it matters. Trust me."

Why wouldn't she just leave things alone? "I think you're wrong. I don't think I can do it, and that means I'm going to let you all down. Eldrick is going to kill me the next time he wants to see where we are. Then I'll be dead. I won't be there to fight by your side. He's going to kill you, too, then. And there's nothing we can do to stop it." I hadn't meant to snap at her, but I just wanted her to leave me alone. Like I said, I didn't want to spend my last hours fighting with her.

Then I heard Cairo echoing in Eva's mind, because she was still connected to me. He said, "Leave him alone. If he wants to sulk, let him, but at least he's flying east. He hasn't given up, so just let him be. Sometimes, people just want to be left alone for a bit."

Her voice in my head was like a roar when she snapped back. "Don't talk about him like that, and don't you dare tell me not to try to comfort my best friend."

"It isn't like that," Cairo said. "I swear I'm not insulting him. Cole is stronger than he knows, but right now, he's not stable. You don't know what he'll do the next time we have to fight or run. I'm worried he's going to do something stupid or dangerous. When he does, I don't want you around him. I don't want you to get hurt."

She snarled. "Why do you care so much? Cole knows me, but you don't. I'm tired of your overprotective attitude, always saying I can't take care of myself. Seems like you don't know me very well, so maybe you should just let me worry about myself."

"Please," he pleaded. It was a new tone, one I hadn't heard from him before. "I just need you to be safe. And you're wrong, I know you better than you think I do. Don't be mad just because people care about you."

Eva didn't respond, but I felt her break contact just before she streaked ahead, sprinting away from me and Cairo.

He started to pull ahead to go after her, but I focused my thoughts at him and said, "Leave her. She just needs some time, trust me. She'll get over it."

Although he didn't shoot ahead, he didn't reply. The whole aura around his mind was full of irritation and...something else. Fear, I thought.

I said, "You don't want to talk, fine. Maybe you can listen, though. You need to tell Eva the truth before it's too late. You know how dangerous things are for us all, but you want to wait, and wait, and wait some more. She deserves to know the truth. You don't even know if we're going to have tomorrow, so I just don't get why you won't tell her today how you feel."

Instead of answering, he cut me off entirely and sped ahead, flying halfway between me and Eva. We spent the next few days spread out like that, each of us lost in our own thoughts. We didn't even speak when we landed to eat and recharge our mahier.

Eventually, we crossed the Bering Strait into Alaska. The sun was just coming up. I spotted a herd of elk and dove after them. Eva and Cairo were right behind me. It was nice to be able to fill up and recharge off just one animal. And it was delicious.

I was the first one to say anything to the others. "So. Here we are in Alaska. Now what?"

"This is your idea" Cairo muttered. "I thought you knew where you were going."

Eva shot him a dirty look. She took in a deep breath, and I could tell she was about to yell at him, when I spotted movement half a mile away in the tree line.

"Be quiet," I said, cutting off her reply.

They both looked at me, irritated.

I continued, "Look there, northeast. In the tree line. Do you see that?"

Cairo blurted, "Carnites. What are they doing here?"

"I count three of them," Eva said. "I wonder where they're going."

I finally had an idea of what to do. I grinned and said, "There's only one thing to do, right? Let's follow them. After you, O brave Eva."

For the first time in days, she smiled. She adjusted her backpack and headed out after them, jogging toward the tree line some distance behind the Carnites.

I shrugged and grinned, then followed her. At last, something to do. I finally felt a hope of finding

Eldrick and our missing allies before I died. As I ran behind her, I kept practicing my mereum shield spell. I really hoped I wouldn't need it any time soon, because it still wasn't working.

Chapter Eighteen

We followed the Carnites through the frozen northern forest. With their long legs and huge size, they moved a lot faster than us, but instead of knocking every tree over, they made their way between them. That slowed them down enough for us to keep up, though just barely. After a half an hour, they reached the top of a hill, then continued down the far side.

When we got to the crest, however, they were nowhere to be seen.

Cairo said, "Stop. Let me see if I can find them." He closed his eyes for about ten seconds, and I could feel the air tingle with his mahier as it spread out, searching for the Carnites. At last, he said, "Down and to your right. They're moving through a ravine."

We ran again, as quickly as we could. After a few minutes, I could hear the Carnites. We followed along atop the ravine rather than trying to climb down into it. If they had any traps, they would be in the ravine, and if they saw us, we would have nowhere to run down there.

A few minutes later, a Carnite's enormous block head appeared through the leaves, then its body, and the next Carnite's head. They were climbing up the other side. They turned eastward, moving away from the ravine and deeper into the forest.

I spat a curse. We were going to have to cross over. I looked at my friends and said, "Dragon?"

They nodded, and we all shifted. It was a little nerve wracking to fly so close to the ground, but if we got up too high, anyone could see us from miles around. Not humans, of course, since we always hid ourselves while flying, but the Carnites and any Elden could see through our illusion if they looked right at us.

Once we got to the other side, we shifted back into our humans and took off after the Carnites. I figured we had been chasing them for about an hour when we heard a crash up ahead.

Cairo called a halt, and we stopped to rest. Maybe they had led us to King Eldrick's camp, but we couldn't be sure. After a few minutes, when we had caught our breath and checked our energy levels, Cairo felt we were ready to creep forward and see whatever we would find.

We crawled forward on our bellies and found a clearing in the forest ahead. There were four Carnites sitting around a bonfire, talking quietly. But no Eldrick and no Elves or Trolls. My heart sank.

Cairo's thoughts came into my mind. "I've been checking my senses, and I don't feel anyone else around. Just these four Carnites. Let's head back a bit so we can talk."

We crept away from the clearing until we were sure they wouldn't see us, then walked a couple minutes more.

I sat on a rock, breathing heavily. "Any ideas? I don't feel Eldrick, whether the Carnites work for him or not. We still need to find him and our friends."

Eva knelt on the forest floor, sitting on her heels, and she just shook her head. No help there. Cairo leaned against a tree and shrugged. It looked like we were out of ideas, for the moment.

Hesitantly, I said, "I suppose we just need to keep following them. I don't think they live in that clearing, so they're going somewhere eventually."

I was startled by an ear-piercing roar from behind us and whipped around to look. A Carnite charged through the forest from the ravine's direction, holding a tree in his right hand like a club. It headed right for Cairo.

I saw shock on Cairo's face, and then he spun to face the noise. The Carnite swung its tree like a golf club, and Cairo stretched out his hand toward it. A crackle of energy zipped through the air as he used his mahier to shield himself from the blow he couldn't dodge. The club smacked him and his barrier crackled. The hit sent him flying through the air toward a tree. Just before he struck it, he held out his other arm to make another barrier. When he hit, the tree snapped in half, but his shield held. Instead of being splattered against the tree, he only tumbled to the ground and came up on his feet. Thankfully, he didn't look injured.

More roars echoed behind us, and I almost panicked when I realized the other Carnites had heard the scream and were charging us from the other direction.

Eva drew her simple, well-crafted sword—Cairo gave his to her when I gave him Jericho's sword—and somersaulted at the first Carnite. She slashed its hip as she went by.

It spun around, swinging its club, but she was already out of range.

Its back was to me, so I sprinted at it, drawing the amazing Mere Blade and thrusting it at the creature's spine. Unlike Jericho's sword, this one slid right through the Carnite's thick hide like butter. It screamed in pain and fell.

We turned toward the other Carnites. Four of them were smashing through the trees, sprinting right at us. Then I heard two more mighty roars from my right and glanced over, only to see another batch of monstrous Carnites. There were only three of us and at least six of them. There was no way we could win this fight. The trees were too dense for us to fly away, and it seemed like we might die before we ever found Eldrick.

The six Carnites stopped when they got close enough to see us, maybe fifty feet away at most, and then spread out. They were trying to cut off any chance of escape, and they could move through that forest faster than any of us if one of us got away. I really didn't want to die in the frozen northern forest, but at least I would be fighting alongside my friends when it happened.

Cairo shouted, "Back-to-back, Keepers."

What else was there to do? Nothing. We formed a circle, facing outward. "It's been an honor, Cairo," I said. "Sorry I got you into this, Eva."

She didn't say anything but grabbed my shoulder and gave me one quick nod. Her simple gesture told me more than words could have, and I felt a lot better about whatever was going to happen next with her at my side. And Cairo's, of course.

The Carnites began stomping their feet and slamming their fists into their chests as they bared their yellow, jagged teeth at us. They towered over us. Suddenly, one Carnite stood up straight and its face went slack. It toppled like a tree, smashing face-first into the ground.

A figure wearing loose clothes and a hood over its face stood on the fallen Carnite's back, its sword in the Carnite's head. It pulled the sword out before sprinting at the next one, sword held overhead with the tip pointed forward.

The other Carnites stopped and looked at their fallen comrade, and if Carnites could look confused, these sure did. I didn't waste any time, though. I charged one of the Carnites, screaming at the top of my lungs.

The next few seconds were a blur. I jumped, I dodged. I somersaulted, I swung my sword. Somewhere along the way, I got hit, but I was so pumped up that I didn't feel it. At least, not at the time. Everything sped by faster than I could keep track of it. It was complete chaos, and at the end, I could hardly tell my friends from my enemies. It was like my mind had just switched off, leaving me to run on instinct. I had a vague impression of doing all sorts of things I didn't know I could, pulling off moves I didn't know I could make.

I pulled my sword from another Carnite and spun, swinging it at something behind me—and only barely managed to stop myself from slashing into Cairo at the last second. We stared at each other for a second, swords held ready to hit each other, and then looked around. I was in a daze, but as I slowly came out of the fog, I saw that all the Carnites were down and Eva and Cairo were still up.

So was the mysterious stranger who had saved us. I walked toward them with a grin, laughing for no reason I could figure out. Maybe I was just happy to be alive, or maybe I was still some kind of battle-crazy.

When I reached the hooded figure, I said, "Thank you so much, friend. You came along just in time. I'm Cole, and these two are Eva and Cairo, my friends. Who are you, what are you doing out here? Not that I'm complaining."

The figure collapsed to the ground, and I rushed to their side. But I froze when the hood slid off, revealing their face.

From behind me, Cairo muttered a curse. There in my arms, lying on the ground with blood trickling from her mouth, was Clara, and she was badly injured.

Chapter Nineteen

As we stood around Clara, Cairo examined her. She had more wounds than I could count, most small but vicious, and two larger wounds. One was a deep gash on her left hip, and the other was the ugliest bruise I had ever seen over her right side. It was clear she had multiple broken ribs.

Cairo said, "Form a circle and grab each other's hands and mine."

We did what he said, and then I felt him drawing power from us. Somehow, the circle seemed to amplify our mahier. I'd experienced that once before, and made a note to ask how it was done. It might come in handy someday.

A faint glow spread over Clara, and as the minutes ticked by, most of her smaller wounds closed before my eyes. The bruise over her side faded, and I actually saw her ribs shift back into place. The largest wound, the gash to her side, closed most of the way, but when the glow faded, it hadn't healed completely, though it wasn't as bad as before.

Cairo answered my question before I asked it. "She took all the healing she can handle, just like Jericho. Any more would hurt her more than help. I think she'll make it now, but she'll be weak for a while."

Her eyelids fluttered open and her eyes darted around. She looked frightened, but when she saw it was us standing over her, her whole body relaxed. I hadn't even realized she was tensed up, ready to strike. She was an impressive warrior.

"Relax, Clara," I said. "You're here with friends. I can't believe how great you were, and you were already really hurt! What happened?"

She closed her eyes and took a couple deep breaths before responding. "Our brother, Eldrick, happened. He's been torturing us all, trying to get us to turn to the darkness. When I refused, the torture just kept going. On and on, and it got worse the more I resisted him."

Cairo's lips turned up into a snarl. He said, "I'm so glad you got away. How did you escape?"

"The whole time, I had been working through the ropes he tied me up with."

She pulled up one sleeve, and despite Cairo's healing, she had scars and ugly, open wounds on her wrist. I could only imagine the ropes sawing their way almost down to her bones.

"At last, he told one of his Elden to just finish me off, then left," she continued. "Me, his sister. I wasn't even important enough to him to watch me die. But I'd worked through one rope just in time, and when the Elden came at me with a knife..."

Cairo nodded, understanding. "You finished him off and used his knife to escape. Thanks to all our ancestors that you're safe, Clara."

She shook her head violently. "No! You don't understand. I'm not safe. You aren't. Ochana isn't safe. He has an army of dark Elves, along with his Elden and half the world's Carnites. And he knows I'm gone. He's going to hunt for me with everything he's got, so I can't warn Ochana."

"Warn us?" I blurted. "About what?" I glanced at Eva, and she met my eyes with the same worry etched on her face.

"About his army. They're on the move against the last group standing in his way."

Cairo growled and then said, "Let him come! Ochana is in his way, and he'd be a fool to attack us now, when we're ready for him."

"That's just it, Cairo. You aren't ready for him. He found a way to get by all your alarms and wards, remember? He'll come in by surprise, and Ochana won't have any warning. It'll be a slaughter if we don't get back there and warn them."

An idea struck me. I hoped it was a good one. "What if we get back and warn Ochana, and instead of waiting for him to hit us, we turn the tables? He doesn't know we know. If we can get our army at him before he leaves Alaska, we can fight them here instead of where it will hurt us. With surprise, maybe we can bring him down once and for all."

Clara nodded and then looked at Cairo. "We should leave right away. But before we go, tell me. What happened to Jericho? Did he make it?"

Cairo's mouth turned up into a faint smile. "Yes, he's alive, but poisoned. We received some weeds from the Mermaids that will heal him. So, relax."

The look that passed between them caught my attention. There was a lot that they weren't saying, I could tell. Elves and dragons hadn't been friends in a long time by my counting, so I was curious. "Why are you asking about Jericho?"

Eva snickered and said, "Maybe they were an item."

Ha. Elves and dragons...as if that could happen. I said, "Don't be silly. That's rude." I couldn't help but smile at her joke, though.

"Actually," Clara said, "you're closer to the truth than you know."

J.A. Culican

Chapter Twenty

I couldn't believe my ears. Jericho and Clara? How could a dragon and an Elf even tolerate each other for long, much less have those kinds of feelings for each other? I thought our kind and theirs just didn't mix, except against a common enemy. But apparently, I had been wrong.

"Can you say that again?" I asked. "It sounded like you said that you and Jericho used to have different kind of feelings for each other."

She sat up and looked at Cairo, but he looked away. "It's true," she said with a sigh. "I started to have feelings for him during the last dragon king's rule, when Ochana took care of dragons and no one else. Jericho had pressed hard for decades to get the dragon king to honor our alliance and come to our help. I respected him for that."

Eva reached out and touched her shoulder. "Let me guess. Respect turned into something more, right?" She rubbed Clara's arm lightly, and I was glad she was there to try to comfort our elven ally.

Clara nodded, and wiped at one eye. "Yes. When I told him how I was confused about my feelings, he told me he felt the same way. He wasn't sure whether it had started before or after he began to press the old dragon king to honor the alliance, though, and that bothered him."

Cairo let out a low whistle. "You mean, he wasn't sure if he wanted Ochana to aid the other races because it was the right thing to do or because of how he felt about you?"

"Yes. For a man like Jericho, you can imagine such a question meant a lot to him. In the end, though, he decided it didn't matter why he had pressed the king to do the right thing, only that he had pressed for honor and duty. We were going to be together, and we'd figure out the problems later."

I was surprised to hear she had feelings for him, but even more surprised to hear he had the same for her—and I was stunned that he had any kind of self-doubt at all. He wasn't just a robot, at least not when it came to Clara. "So, what happened? Why aren't you two living happily ever after?"

She didn't answer right away, looking at the ground like she was trying to figure out what to say, or how to say it. I think we sat like that, all looking at Clara, for half a minute before she finally said, "It was when Jago died. Rylan became the king, and he made Jericho the lead Woland for all Ochana, all in one day. Jericho had new duties, and he became obsessed with finding out what happened to his best and only true friend. And then, there were my own people..."

Cairo interjected immediately. "When the dragons tried to rejoin the world, the Elves again thought of us. And they were angry. Suddenly, they would have noticed if you were spending time with a dragon. They would have been enraged. Does that sum it up?"

Clara nodded and wiped at her eyes again. "Yes. We both decided to go our separate ways for the good of our people. But it was stupid. We never should have walked away. How often do you get to really love someone? Why should it matter that he's a dragon and I'm an Elf? I love him anyway, and as close as I just came to death, I see things differently now. I want to be with him, no matter what it costs me. Even for our kind, life is too short to sacrifice something as important as your heart. I'll find a way to be with him again, I swear I will."

We comforted her, and she fell asleep a little later. We prepared to make the run to Ochana. As we packed our things, Cairo hovered near Eva, and I wondered what he was going to do. He took a deep breath, and then he walked right up to her.

"Eva, listen. Hearing Clara's tale has put my mind right. I need to tell you something."

"Cairo, this isn't really the best—"

He cut her off, saying, "No, it can't wait. I...I have feelings for you. No, it's more than that, I love you. I'm in love with you. Among our kind, we call it *Vera Salit*, and it means soulmates. Destined by Fate to be together. I wish I'd told you sooner, and Cole tried to make me, but I was too afraid. I said it was because the timing wasn't right, but the truth wasn't so noble."

"Stop! Just stop talking, Cairo." Eva's face turned angry.

I was stunned. I couldn't look away—it was like a train wreck.

"How dare you tell me this now, when Clara almost died and Ochana is in danger? Get your head in the game, Cairo."

His expression fell. I thought he might get upset, but he wasn't done trying yet. "You're wrong. There's no better time than now. I couldn't live with myself if something happened to you before I had a chance to tell you."

"I said stop it, Cairo. There's no such thing as soulmates. People meet, they love, they stop loving, they move on. It's the way the world runs."

"No, you're wrong. What about when you were kidnapped? We never should have found you, but we did. That was Fate guiding us. Or what about when you first turned into the Golden Dragon? Think back. You know I'm right. Maybe it's so rare that no one really believes it, but you and me, we feel it. *Vera Salit*. Destiny. Tell me I'm wrong, Eva! If you're honest with yourself, you can't say it."

I saw the anger drain from her face when he mentioned finding her when she'd been kidnapped. When he mentioned the Golden Dragon transformation, she finally looked up at him and met his gaze. Slowly, she began to nod. She said, "I don't know. Yes, I feel...something. And when you said *Vera Salit*, I felt a jolt shoot up my spine, like the word had some power."

Cairo let out a relieved sigh. He smiled briefly, and put his hand on her shoulder. "That's your mahier recognizing the truth when it hears it. I'm right. *Now* we can do what needs doing, and if anything happens to me, I won't die having never told you."

Eva was actually blushing a little, which I didn't often see. It was hard to fluster her. She said, "I feel it, too, even though I didn't want to hear it. But now what?"

She took a step toward him, and I figured they were going to kiss, so I looked at Clara. She was watching the two with a smile.

Then Cairo said, "Now, I have to go warn Ochana about the attack, before it's too late."

Eva blurted out, "Wait. What? You can't go now. You just told me some cosmic reality about true love being real, and you want to leave? Let me come with you, at least!"

"I'm sorry, Eva, but with the dark Elf army running around somewhere out there, it's too dangerous. You're the Keeper of Dragons, too, and if something happens to you, all is lost. Stay with Cole—you're safer together. If I'm lucky, I'll get the dragons to come here to stop Eldrick's attack before it starts. And it's time to tell the Mermaids. They promised warriors, and we're going to need them. I swear I'll be back as fast as I can." He summoned his dragon as he jumped into the air, transitioning in a blink, and flew up and away.

Eva stood with her jaw dropped. Tears welled up in her eyes.

I couldn't leave her like that; she was my best friend. "Eva, he's right. Clara is still too weak to travel, and we can't abandon her here with Eldrick searching for her. He'll be back as fast as any dragon ever could be, I promise. He's been talking about this soulmate stuff for a while, now. I think he'd move the sky and the moon to get back to you."

She didn't say anything, just wrapped her arms around me and buried her face in my shoulder. She was usually the strong, brave one. I think she was feeling something she hadn't ever felt before and didn't know how to handle it. I let her cry softly until she was done, then we rejoined Clara. It made me wish I had a soulmate of my own, but how often could that *Vera Salit* thing happen, if it was practically a myth?

Chapter Twenty-One

We let Clara get a good night's sleep, and in the morning, she felt much better. She still had to hobble a little, but given how urgent it was to find the Elves and Trolls being held prisoner, she insisted she was well enough to travel. Eva and I didn't argue.

Besides, if we hung out there until Clara healed up more, Eldrick would find us. There was no doubt he had minions searching for her, so at first light, we headed out across the frozen Alaska forest.

"It was pretty close. I wasn't able to run very far with the wounds he gave me. In fact, I was about to collapse when I heard your fight with the Carnites."

Eva replied, "I don't think it was a coincidence you found us. Fate led you to us. I'm glad you came along, too, because I don't think we would have made it without you."

Clara shrugged and smiled. "I know I wouldn't have made it without you, so we're even."

As we trudged through the snowy forest, I found myself walking between them. We all ended up chatting and joking. I thought it was the first time I had seen Clara really open up. I figured saving each other's lives made it easier to let our guards down, despite the bad blood between Elves and dragons. I hoped it would make the Elven Alliance even stronger.

After a couple hours, we reached the forest's outer edge. The snow was deeper, but we no longer had to go around trees, climb over logs, or untangle backpacks from creeper vines and snagging bushes. We ended up moving even faster, despite the heavier snow.

"Hey," I said, "does anyone else notice the snow isn't blinding you? I thought it was supposed to be a thing. 'Snow blind.' But it just seems like normal daylight."

Clara laughed at me, and I blushed. She said, "Don't be embarrassed. You haven't been in touch with your dragon for long. Once you reached your teens, your eyes adjust to light like a dragon's. Bright light doesn't blind you unless it's sudden, like a flare. Cool, huh?"

I agreed, it was pretty cool. I wondered what else I didn't have to worry about. Maybe I couldn't freeze to death, either. I hoped not—it was bitterly cold out here, especially when the breeze picked up.

Clara pointed ahead and a bit to the right. "There it is."

I turned to look where she pointed, and my eyes grew wide as saucers. There was a huge castle, right in the middle of Alaska. "Wow. Is that really what I think it is?"

She grinned and nodded. "It's an old Elven family holding. We haven't been there in years, so we had no idea the Elden had taken it over. It's huge, though."

"A castle is awesome and all, but how are we supposed to get in?" Eva asked. "Do they leave the drawbridge down or something?"

I was so distracted by the castle that I didn't notice when Clara stopped walking, and I almost ran into her. "Why did we stop?" I asked.

"Eva asks a good question."

"What do you mean?" Eva set her backpack down and stretched her back and shoulders.

Clara let her pack slide off, too. "The thing is impossible to get inside. The fortifications are impregnable. Also, it's in the middle of a huge lake."

That wasn't what I wanted to hear. "Wait a minute. If it's impossible to get into, how did you escape? If there's a way out, there has to be a way in."

Eva said, "Unless they blocked off the way she got out. That's what I'd do if I were Eldrick."

That did make sense. "So, what now?"

Clara smirked, looking like the cat that ate the canary. "I escaped through a door hidden in a wall, and I'm sure they've blocked that off by now. But I know something Eldrick doesn't. There's an entire system of tunnels running under both the castle and lake. I don't know it all, but I know how to get in and how to get to the castle. I can lead us through it."

Eva snapped her fingers, looking suddenly excited. "That's perfect! Once we get the Elves and Trolls loose, we have to get them out, right? We can just lead them back through the tunnels. With any luck, the Elden won't even know they're gone until it's too late."

I said, "I think they'll notice so many people moving around. They have to have guards watching the prisoners."

"Not if we can give them some sort of a distraction," Eva said. "If we can do something big enough, they won't be looking at the prisoners. That would be the perfect time to try to sneak them out."

That wasn't such a bad idea, actually. "I wonder if showing up at their gate would be enough of a distraction."

She shook her head. "I had something bigger in mind. This castle may have walls no one could get through, surrounded by a lake no one can get across, but that won't stop a dragon. I think when Cairo gets back with the dragon Realms, we can all give them the biggest distraction anyone ever saw. They could attack the castle itself from above while we rescue the Elves and Trolls."

I felt a little embarrassed. "Of course. I don't know why I didn't think of that. I'm just not used to thinking of things from a dragon's point of view, I guess."

"That won't work," Clara said. "Who knows how many decades or centuries Eldrick has had to build up the magical defenses around the castle? They were pretty strong to begin with, and he's had nothing but time to make them even stronger."

Eva grinned, wide enough to show her teeth. "Yeah, but you're forgetting about the Mere Treaty. The Mermaids can swim in the lake, maybe even help the Elves and Trolls to escape, but we can have them focus on breaking down the magical defenses so the troops can attack it."

Clara looked surprised. "You recruited the Mermaids? I can't believe it. The Mermaids stick to themselves even more than the dragons used to. That's fantastic news. I doubt Eldrick is making plans to deal with Mere magic."

I replied, "Yes, it was tough, but we got them to agree to join the alliance."

She looked relieved. "That might make all the difference. Mermaid magic is strong, and mereum isn't the same as mahier and tilium. It could even be the strongest magic there is, but it's also the slowest. That's perfect for bringing down the castle's defenses."

I rubbed my chin, thinking. "If Eldrick didn't think the Mermaids were joining us, then he hasn't had time to put in new magic against them, right?"

She nodded. "That sums it up."

I slid my backpack off and sat on a rock. "Now all we have to do is wait for Cairo and the dragon army. Then we can launch our surprise attack. The Mermaid queen taught me how to get in touch with her, and she said they would be ready for our call. As soon as we update Cairo, we can get the rescue started."

We only had to wait for about an hour before dark specks appeared in the sky on the horizon. I tried to count the specks, but there were too many. It was the dragons! More of them than I had ever seen before. I jumped to my feet and cheered their arrival. I cheered even louder when Jericho was the first to land. The plant must have worked.

Happy to see Jericho once again, I took a step to go greet him, but just then, my head reeled. I staggered as I felt another vision coming on, then toppled over.

Queen Desla's words flashed through my mind when I hit the ground: *"...If you have another vision, you'll die..."*

Chapter Twenty-Two

I fell to my hands and knees, snarling in frustration. If Eldrick found us, our cover would be blown and the element of surprise would be lost, just like the battle. And I definitely didn't want to die out here in the snow.

I pushed back against the vision, using all of my strength with both my mahier and tilium. No matter how hard I pressed, though, Eldrick's strength was greater. I could feel him pushing toward my mind, crushing my magic shell as he came closer and closer. His piercing thoughts drove like a nail straight toward my brain, pushing all my power aside. I grew desperate and frantically shoved back at him. He budged, but only slightly, and it wasn't enough. I couldn't keep this up for long, I knew.

My vision was black, but as though from a great distance, a light came toward me. I realized it must be Eldrick's latest vision, coming for me. My tilium was gone, my mahier was almost gone. When that flickered, the vision suddenly sprinted toward me even faster.

At the last second, I threw up all my remaining mahier. I had stopped the vision, but I was sweating with the effort. My strength was about to give out; there wasn't any way I could stop him. I was doomed.

Then, through the deep blackness I was floating in, I heard a voice, Eva's voice, and her soft and welcome whisper echoed all around me. It seemed to be coming from everywhere at once, and nowhere.

"Cole, fight it. You can do it, I have faith in you. You're not alone, I'm here with you. Cairo is here, and Jericho. Clara is here, and Desla. We are all around you right now, so fight!"

In her voice, I heard the love and friendship we shared. I felt warmth and strength flowing through me because of the love and trust they had for me. All of my friends standing around me felt a little different.

Memories shot through my mind like movie screens, whizzing by. Each one was a scene from my life. The day Eva and I met. The first time she stood up for me at school. Rylan and Sila telling me they loved me and had faith in me. Jericho spending long, frustrating hours training me. Desla, teaching me how to use and gather mereum to protect myself from Eldrick's magic.

And then, last of all, one flickering movie screen stopped for a just a heartbeat, right in front of me—my adopted parents on the day I left them, wrapping their arms around me and crying. *"We love you, Cole. No matter where you go, this is your home. You'll always be in our hearts, son."*

Eva was right. They were all right. I could do this. I was the Keeper of Dragons. The Fates picked me for this moment, right? It was my destiny to beat him, even when all seemed lost. To save the dragons, my parents, and my friends. To save the world from the Time of Fear.

I felt the water in the air around me, in the vast lake nearby, in the trees and plants that grew from that water. Power was everywhere, surrounding me, more than I could ever need. I drew it into myself, feeling its essence.

My flickering mahier flared into life, shining bright in the darkness. It pushed away the vision Eldrick was trying to hammer me with. First an inch, then a foot, I pushed him away from me, away from my friends, away from my people. There was a loud *crack*, like a thunderbolt, and I knew it was his rage. I shoved him from my mind like he was just a leaf blowing in a typhoon.

The darkness faded. When my sight came back, everyone stood around me, supporting me. I looked up and grinned. I had done it.

***

Jericho beamed down at me as I climbed to my feet. He was usually angry like fire or just withdrawn, but now he didn't hesitate to wrap his arms around me in a warm embrace. "Thank Aprella you're all right," he said. "I never would have forgiven myself if anything happened to you while I was ill. Those leaves you brought back...the three of you saved my life. Thank you."

"I'm just glad you made it. I didn't have any faith that a bunch of leaves could fix you up, but here you are. I'm glad I listened to you."

He grinned at me. "Yes, for once. Hopefully, it becomes a habit."

Then Eva barreled into me, wrapping her arms around me. I looked into her eyes and couldn't help but smile. "Hello, there."

She wiped one eye and said, "Don't you ever scare me like that again. I thought we were gonna lose you."

**

After my magic battle with Eldrick, I was starving. They led me back to our makeshift camp, where they stacked tray after tray in front of me, loaded down with food. Once, I would've thought it was too much, but I knew better now. I dug in like I was really starving to death.

255

As I nibbled the last bits of meat off a rib, I looked around at the camp. It was fairly impressive, but half of it was empty. Maybe that was for the Mermaids when they arrived.

Cairo stood at the tree line with Eva. They faced one another, their bodies stiff and their arms straight at their sides. I smiled to myself, recognizing the nervousness they felt.

Cairo reached out and took Eva's hands in both of his and pulled her to him. He wrapped his arms around her. They stood like that for a minute, then he kissed her on her forehead and walked into the forest, pulling a smiling Eva after him. I was sure they had plenty to talk about before the battle, and I hoped they both made it through it. I didn't know what would happen to a *Vera Salit* if their soulmate died.

But then, Jericho walked up to me on my left, and Clara came up on my right. It wasn't until they got pretty close that they both stopped mid-step to stare at each other, looking surprised. That was interesting; taking a few steps back, I watched them.

Just out of earshot, Jericho talked softly to her. They both looked nervous. He kept scratching the back of his neck, and she grabbed her left elbow with her other hand.

I shook my head a little, not really sure what to do about it. If those two cared about each other so much, they should be together, even if they were from different people. Just because he was a dragon and she was an Elf didn't mean they couldn't be together, right? It seemed simple to me. Then again, I hadn't grown up in their cultures, with the bad feelings that simmered between Elves and dragons. I only hoped they'd figure it out before it was too late.

I grew bored of watching them whisper to each other, so I got busy finishing my food. A couple hours later, I felt like my old self again. I wandered off and found Cairo.

He grabbed me by the arm and pulled me to the side.

I looked around the field and saw two great armies, dragons on one side and Mermaids on the other. They must have arrived while I was eating everything in sight. I couldn't imagine Eldrick fighting off so many of us, but then again, he had beaten the Elves and Trolls together, stolen their tilium, taken down Paraiso, and done half a dozen other impossible things. Plus, we had no idea how many of Earth's dark races he had gathered as allies. Maybe we were outnumbered, for all I knew.

Cairo said, "You have to talk to the commanders. Desla, Jericho and Jude, and Clara, who's leading what's left of the Elves and Trolls. Plus the Fairy queen, since she managed to gather all the scattered Fairies together."

I grinned at him and he raised an eyebrow, looking confused. I said, "It's like the Battle of Five Armies. Our four and Eldrick's. Hopefully it ends with us winning, just like in the book."

He grinned. "I trust our Book of Aprella more than the book you mean. Ours says you're going to win."

"Good point." I chuckled.

I waited until Eva let me know the commanders were all together, then I walked into the tent with Eva at my side. I was nervous talking to so many commanders and members of royalty at once, but they all looked at me with bright, hopeful eyes when I came in. It turned out that, since it was she and I destined to drive back the Time of Fear, we'd be the ones in charge, too. I knew I couldn't let them down.

I told them our plan to use the tunnels to rescue the Elves and Trolls, and what we needed them each to do. Together, we worked out the details. Maybe we could have planned it better, but we didn't have time to get fancy with it. The Mermaids would take over the lake and hammer away at the castle's magic defenses, the dragons of Realm Five would swoop in with a surprise attack from above, and then the last part. Clara would bring Eva, Jericho, and me through the underground tunnel system. I hated the idea of being underground in those tunnels, but it was the best we could come up with.

Just as the sun went down, we broke up so the commanders could go instruct their armies, and Clara led us to the tunnel entrance. It looked just like a mouth, too, ready to swallow us up. I took a deep breath and followed Clara inside just as the battle above began.

J.A. Culican

Chapter Twenty-Three

I looked around at my little group, burning their faces into my memory in case any of us died on our mission. Clara and Jericho stood arm-in-arm, while Eva and Cairo stood so close together that their arms touched.

"Clara, I think we're ready. We'll follow you through the tunnels until we reach the middle of the castle. If you haven't found the prisoners by then, we'll come up underneath and see what we can do to help in the battle up there, while you keep searching." Jericho instructed.

"Follow me." She led us a short distance away, stopping at a large boulder. Then she stretched her arms wide to both sides and muttered under her breath. I couldn't understand what she said, but the words sounded beautiful, like a bird singing.

As she spoke, the rock's flat face began to glow, and a pattern started to shine. It started as a Celtic knot, and little tendrils of light twisted and turned, racing along as more and more of the knot work could be seen. At the end, the entire knot formed a beautiful, huge, door-shaped glyph. It suddenly flared bright enough to hurt my eyes, pulsated, and then in one last, bright flash, the entire glyph vanished. It left behind an archway with stairs going down. A cool, wet breeze blew out from the tunnel, smelling of rock and dust.

"Stay close to each other," she said. "These tunnels go on forever. It's one huge maze. If you get separated, I may not be able to find you. We don't have time to stop and look for anyone, either."

Cairo said, "So, what you're saying is, don't get lost?"

She smiled and nodded, then turned and headed down the stone stairs into the darkness below.

Once we were in the dark tunnel, I noticed small symbols all along the walls, and whenever anyone got within a few feet of one, it lit up. The tunnel branches all looked the same to me, which made me nervous. I was even more nervous when we left the main tunnel we had come in on. Instead, Clara led us to the left, then the right. We skipped a few doorways and then turned left again. Right, right again, and another two left turns. If anything happened to our guide, I'd be hopelessly lost.

I think we had been walking for almost an hour when the narrow tunnel opened up into a huge chamber. The floor here had been chiseled smooth, and the ceiling was smooth and high, maybe thirty feet above us. Scattered all through the chamber, stretching away into the darkness, stone pillars held up the ceiling. From what I could see, the room had been carved *around* the pillars, and they were all one stone with the ceiling and floor.

Clara stepped out onto that floor and all around her, the outline of a complicated symbol lit up, just like in the tunnels, but it stretched away and faded into the darkness. She stepped aside for the rest of us to come out of the tunnel, and wherever anyone stepped on the chamber floor, the outlines in the symbol lit up.

"So much for sneaking up on anyone," Jericho grumbled.

"Yes, that's going to be hard," Clara said. "We need to get through this chamber, though. There's another tunnel on the opposite side, just like the one we left, which takes us up into the castle."

I said, "Let's get moving, then. The war isn't waiting for us." I smiled at her and she grinned back, then she headed out across the chamber.

It was nerve-wracking the way the chamber stretched off into darkness in every direction, like I could easily get lost in a big, dark, featureless sea of stone. I was glad Clara seemed to know the way.

We had been making our away slowly across the floor, staying between one row of pillars. I couldn't keep my eyes off them, because every time we passed one, different symbols lit up in a pale blue light, and I could almost make sense of them. It was like each glyph showed one thing, but together, they told a story. I really wished I could understand the writing.

Ahead, I heard someone screech. I recognized Clara's voice. I scrambled forward, and saw everyone standing together, staring ahead. I followed their gaze to see what they were looking at.

My jaw dropped. Up ahead were rows after rows of iron cages, and in each one sat an Elf or a Troll. None of the cages were tall enough for them to stand up, and I could only imagine the pain of sitting on those iron bars this entire time without being able to stretch out, even.

Jericho muttered, "By Aprella..."

I was awestruck. I hadn't realized Eldrick had taken so many people. Then I realized these weren't even all of them, just the ones who hadn't turned dark yet. The army Eldrick must have gathered from them was stunning.

"Let's get them out of there before Eldrick realizes we're here," I said.

Clara and Jericho wasted no time. They stormed up to the cages and held their hands to the locks, one after the other. Each time they did, there was a flash of light and then the door creaked open. If only the Elves and Trolls still had their tilium, they could have easily released themselves. It made me angry and sad just looking at them, locked up like that.

I hurried after the others and got busy undoing locks. It turned out to be easy with mahier—just will it to open, and it did.

The prisoners started to climb out, but they moved slowly because their legs and backs were cramped from sitting so long. Before they could get out, though, all the doors slammed shut at once. It made a deafening *clang*. I looked around in surprise.

A terrible cackle echoed through the chamber. The noise bounced off the walls and pillars, making it impossible to tell where it came from. Then a deep voice in the darkness said, "You didn't think I knew where Clara was? I may not have been able to follow the Keeper, but once she escaped, I knew she'd be back. I knew she'd come through these tunnels."

Clara shouted back, "That's why you didn't send anyone after me?"

"You fool. You've walked into my trap, and even better, you brought the Keepers with you. Soon this will all be over, and the Earth will be mine."

Across the darkness in every direction, we saw lights coming. Dozens and dozens, all streaming toward us. Elden, and they'd be on top of us in moments.

Jericho shouted, "To arms! Stand back to back!"

Clara's high-pitched, beautiful voice rang out and said, "No! Run, back the way we came. We can come back later. There are too many of them."

In a panic, we all ran, but we only got a few steps before dozens more lights flared up, coming toward us from the direction of the escape tunnel.

"Is there another tunnel?" I asked. "Better lost than dead."

Clara nodded and ran off into the darkness in the only direction we saw no enemy lights. After a minute, we reached the chamber's wall, but it was smooth and unbroken.

I said, "Where are the tunnels?"

She shook her head. "They should be here! He must have closed them."

Jericho drew his sword. "Then get your backs to the wall. They're almost on us, and we're going to have to fight our way out."

That was wishful thinking. Eldrick's soldiers were close enough now that I could make out some of their faces. Some were Elden, others were dark Elves, but there were way too many of them. I drew the Mere Blade, the sword Desla had given me. It glowed brightly. At least I would take as many of them with us as I could.

I said, "Eva, I'm sorry I got you into this."

She grunted, then said, "There's no one I'd rather be fighting next to. We tried to save the world, but win or lose, what mattered is that we tried."

Eldrick's voice rang out again, laughing. "No, what matters is that you died. Soon, friends, I'll dance on your bodies."

The huge crowd of Elden and dark Elves had surrounded us, but a bunch of them in the middle stepped aside to let Eldrick come through. He stopped just outside of striking distance and grinned.

I readied myself to try to charge at him. This was my chance. Maybe I could take him with us.

Chapter Twenty-Four

Eldrick and his forces barreled toward us. He had a sneer on his face, his lips curled up to bare his teeth. As his soldiers rushed us, he threw his head back and laughed, and the menacing sound echoing through the chamber sent a shiver down my spine.

He held his hand up when they were just about to smash into us, and they stopped and backed up. He looked at us for a long moment without saying anything, but then he said, "I could just kill you all at once, but that seems so much less satisfying than killing you one at a time. Just watching the looks on your faces as one friend after another dies on my blade sounds entertaining. You all irritate me, after all, and where would be the justice in killing you all at once?"

I knew he meant it, too. In my mind, I ran through one plan after another, but had to toss each aside. They wouldn't work.

Maybe I couldn't save us all, but I thought I might be able to save some of my friends. I raised my chin at him and shouted, "I don't honestly think you want to kill your sister, and the rest of these people simply did what I told them. I'm the Keeper of Dragons, after all. Why don't you let them go and just take me? When they see what you do to me, all your enemies will know they've been beaten. Kill their spirits, their hope, and let them live with that. That's the ultimate punishment."

"Cole, no, don't do it!" Eva cried.

Eldrick locked eyes with me. He brought one hand up and stroked his chin, making a big show of considering my offer. That's when I knew he was going to say no. It had been a long shot anyway, though.

He said, "Or—and I'm just throwing ideas out, here—why don't I just kill all of them one by one *and then* torment you? I think it's a better ending than letting them go, don't you think?"

He was right, it would be a worse thing than just torturing me and letting them go. I didn't have an answer for him, but nothing I said would have changed his mind anyway.

I fixed my grip on the Mere Blade and got ready for the fighting to start.

"Elden, wait!" Eldrick shouted. "I think I'll kill Jericho first. Attack the rest, but don't kill them, yet. I want them to see them die."

He got a gleam in his eye and strolled toward Jericho while the Elden swarmed toward the rest of us, and the fight was on.

My sword cut through the Elden weapons as easily as it cut through them. I didn't know how many I killed, three or four at least, but even so, they managed to cut us off from Jericho. He had to fight Eldrick alone.

The Elden stopped pressing their attack. They stood between us and Jericho, and there was nothing we could do to help him. We could only watch in horror as he fought Eldrick one-on-one.

Eldrick thrust, but Jericho blocked it and then lunged. He batted Jericho's sword aside and, in one smooth movement, came around with a backhanded slash. His sword left a deep cut on the dragon's left arm, above the elbow.

Jericho roared in pain and lunged again, but Eldrick blocked the attack and his blade missed by an inch. Eldrick swept his blade downward, and left another cut on Jericho's right thigh. This time, Jericho cried out in pain and staggered back. He was wounded, and I could see he was slowing down. I thought the fight would be over soon and fought the urge to try to cut my way through all those Elden to go help my friend. I knew that would have been suicide, though.

Eldrick laughed. He had started to toy with Jericho, adding more cuts but not really trying to kill the dragon. My blood boiled. He said, "And so falls the mighty Jericho, so-called guardian of Ochana. How pathetic."

He lunged forward and there was a quick flash of blades coming together—but then Jericho was disarmed, his blade skittering a few feet away on the smooth rock floor. Eldrick raised his blade above his head and, cackling like a madman, rushed at Jericho to deliver a killing blow.

Clara cried out wordlessly, the most anguished and painful sound I think I'd ever heard, like her soul was being torn apart. She held her hand out at Eldrick and Jericho as if that would somehow stop him, and I closed my eyes. I didn't want to see any of it, not Jericho dying, and not her dying inside. But I peeked anyway—I couldn't help it.

And yet, it did stop him. His blade came sweeping down in a deadly arc toward Jericho's head, but inches away, the blade stopped like it had hit a rock. There was a flare, blindingly bright, and at first, I thought Clara had put some sort of a shield up over Jericho. I think all of our jaws must have dropped when we saw that. But I gasped in shock when I realized the bright light covered not Jericho, but Eldrick and all of his soldiers, too.

Clara screamed, rage and fear in her voice. "No! I'll kill you, brother. Today, you die here." Light streamed from her hand toward Eldrick and his soldiers. It got brighter and brighter, and then began to push them back as she swept her hand to one side—moving him away from Jericho. I had no idea what she was doing and had never heard of anything like it. From Jericho's shocked expression, I could see he'd never seen it, either.

Eldrick and the Elden wasted no time. They began to hack furiously at the light that surrounded them. Then one of the soldier's blades shattered when it struck the barrier. Eldrick snarled and screamed in rage.

I felt a tug at my sleeve and looked over. It was Eva. She whispered, "Come on, now's your chance. Let's free the Elves and Trolls."

We took off, working our way around the blinding light that held the Elden away. I got to the first cage and put my hand over the lock, willing it to open. There was a brief, faint glow and a click, and the door open. One after the other, Eva and I let the prisoners escape.

Nearby, there was an area that looked like it was for guards, with weapons racks and shelves full of supplies. One of the Elves bashed open the locks, then began throwing every sort of weapon to the other Elves and Trolls as they escaped. Soon, we had a dozen or more armed new friends. Some joined Clara and Cairo, but the others kept passing out swords and spears while Eva and I released more of our captured allies.

I realized then that, when Clara's shield failed or she ran out of tilium, it wouldn't matter—the enemy was outnumbered. The only way out for them was to go back the way they had come, up into the castle.

Eldrick must have realized that, too, because he stopped trying to slash through the shield and shouted for the Elden to retreat. They fled away from us and headed toward the stairwell that would lead them up into the castle.

Cairo shouted, "They're getting away. Clara, bring down the shield."

"I can't! I don't know how I did it in the first place or how to bring it down."

Unfortunately, her barrier blocked us from pursuing Eldrick. We could only stand and watch as he ran. It only took a couple minutes for Clara's tilium to be drained, but by then our enemy was long gone.

Jericho shouted, and then there was a commotion. I turned to look just as Clara collapsed.

He caught her before she hit the ground and gently lowered her, resting her head in his lap.

I made my way through the freed Elves to join Cairo watching them. Clara looked terrible. Her cheeks were sunken and her eyes were dark with huge bags under them. She tried to talk, but nothing came out.

Jericho said, "Hush, save your strength. Please, just lay still."

The corners of Clara's mouth turned up into a weak smile. She took a deep breath and then, with great effort, said in a feeble voice, "I've always known how you felt about me, Jericho."

"That doesn't matter now," he said. "You need to save your strength. What can we do to help?"

She reached up with one trembling hand and placed her fingertips on his cheek. "It does matter, more than anything. You've loved me, and I have always loved you even before you told me how you felt. Nothing has changed over the years. I wish I had been brave enough to tell you."

He leaned down, and she wrapped her arms around his neck as he planted his lips on hers.

Feeling awkward, I looked away. They deserved privacy. Those two had loved each other for decades, or maybe centuries, and they had been too stubborn to say it, too afraid to take a chance on their love for one another. They both had to almost die to make them realize that none of us have forever, and we might not even have tomorrow. I was happy to let them show each other how they felt after all that time.

A few seconds later, I heard Jericho standing, so I looked back over. He was helping Clara stand, and Cairo rushed forward to grab her other arm. Together, they got her to her feet. She was still weak, but she could finally stand.

I looked around the room and saw all the Elves and Trolls were armed, and there were so many of them that we had a small army of our own. We could throw them into the battle going on in the castle above us, and maybe even make a difference.

"Jericho, Eldrick is getting away," I said. "There's a battle going on right over our heads. Lead us up into the castle. I think a new army hitting the defenders by surprise ought to make quite a difference, don't you?"

He turned and barked some orders, and quickly got the Elves and Trolls divided into smaller units. He put two of the smaller squads under each of us— Eva, Cairo, Clara, himself, and me—and we rushed toward the stairwell, out of the dungeon, and up into the castle.

What I saw when I came up into the light of day was a total surprise. There was still fighting going on, but it was clustered into little knots. There were enough bodies to account for the rest, and it was clear we'd almost taken the castle. Whatever Elden and dark Elves still lived must have fled with Eldrick.

Eva turned and wrapped her arms around me, burying her face in my shoulder. She muttered, "It's over. We saved the Elves and Trolls, and now it's over. We can go back to our lives."

I wasn't so sure about that. Eldrick was still alive after all, but I let her have her moment.

All around us, Elves, Trolls, and everyone else roared, cheering their great victory.

Chapter Twenty-Five

Once the battle was over and the last few Elden had been swept away by swords and flames, our army celebrated. I was happy to join them. At long last, the threat was over, Eldrick was defeated, and we could all get on with our lives.

Somewhere during all that celebrating, dozens more dragons showed up carrying a feast of food, and the lakeshore camp turned into one big victory party. It had been a close battle, and only Eldrick running away in the middle had guaranteed our win. Everyone there had fought and they'd earned a celebration as far as I was concerned.

After I'd had plenty to eat and regained my spent mahier, Cairo and Eva found me while I was listening to a Mere soldier talking about the battle.

"C'mon," Cairo said. "I guess there's going to be a meeting inside and they want you and Eva there, too."

I shook hands with the soldier and followed Cairo into the castle. Once out in the courtyard, I was greeted by Prince Gaber and Queen Annabelle. King Evander of the Trolls, Queen Desla, and Jericho were also there waiting for us.

Gaber said, "Now that the Keepers are here, let's all take a seat. We have much to discuss."

There were a dozen chairs nearby, so I grabbed one. We arranged ourselves in a little circle, which I thought was appropriate. Without a table, no one could be at the head. It was just another sign that the alliance was getting stronger. That was a good thing, because I was sure that although the Elden had been chased off, there were still plenty of enemies in the world.

Annabelle cleared her throat and then said, "Fighting together, we've taken a great victory here today, yet there is still much work to be done. Most of the Elves still don't have their tilium. Eldrick is on the loose, still working with the Carnites. He has two armies under him, the Elden and the dark Elves. So many of them escaped, they could still cause problems."

"I think we have little to fear from him," Jericho said. "The Elven Alliance stands as strong as it ever did, and the dragons will keep working to restore the trust we once had. We went down the wrong path under our old king, but Rylan has always valued our alliances."

Desla stood to speak, shaking her head. "There is still a lot of bad blood between the other races and dragons. Today went a long way toward healing old wounds, but don't make the mistake of thinking that trust is regained because you joined us for one battle. And Eldrick is a master of taking advantage of hidden resentments no one else may even see. He has always seemed able to find the weak points—as any Elf can tell you."

I wasn't sure why everyone seemed so pessimistic. Well, not Jericho, but probably all the others. It was a little frustrating. I said, "I agree. The alliance is stronger than it has been a long time, and it does still have problems. But I promise you, the dragons won't rest until they fix the damage they did. Anyway, why do we need to talk about these problems right now? We beat Eldrick and he's on the run. All of us will hunt him around the globe, right?"

Jericho said, "It's only a matter of time until we find him and finish what we started here."

"Definitely. And for the first time since I found out I was a dragon, I don't have this ball of worry in my gut saying everything is hopeless. Now, I see the hope. I think lots of people will agree."

Eva smiled at me, and I could tell she agreed.

I continued, "I know we need to strengthen the alliance, because there's always going to be another threat down the road. But the Time of Fear is over, right? For now, I think we should all just take one great big sigh of relief. Just let our people party together like they used to. The more we do that, the less damage Eldrick can do before we finally hunt him down once and for all." I slammed my fist into my other palm as I said that.

Jericho nodded at me, and I could see approval in his expression. I think that look was the best part of my day, besides helping to free the prisoners. "And that day—"

I thought I heard a strange noise and stopped talking. I cocked my head, trying to listen. Then I realized what it was—there was a growing roar coming from our army's camp. At first, I worried it was some new threat, but then I heard a clear victory cheer.

"What's going on out there, do you think?" Gaber asked.

Jericho shook his head. "There's only one way to find out. I say we take a break and go see."

We got up and headed toward the drawbridge. Once we stepped out onto those old, thick timbers, I saw the mob of soldiers in the field, making a path for... What? I squinted, trying to see well, and caught sight of people coming out of the woods bordering the camp.

Gaber shouted with excitement, his voice rising into something like a cheer. I looked at him, confused. He met my eyes and said, "I can't believe it. It's the ancestors! They've returned! That can only mean our tilium will be coming back soon, too. They wouldn't have come out if our victory hadn't been total."

Jericho grinned, baring his teeth like a predator and said, "Proof that Eldrick is finished. He just doesn't know it yet."

That's when the party really got going. It lasted long into the night.

***

We were flying back to Ochana and all the dragons were in high spirits. Eva and I flew side-by-side, talking excitedly about the battle and everything that had happened. When the dragon flying in front of me stopped, I almost crashed right into her, but I stopped short at the last second. I saw Jericho hovering, long neck hanging down as he looked at something below us.

I tried to see what he was looking at. There was a black spot way below, on the ground. It had to be really big for us to see it from so high up. I flew over to him and asked, "Is that normal? I haven't seen anything like that before."

He looked up. "No, Cole, that is definitely not normal. I don't know what it is."

I had an itch at the back of my mind that I couldn't scratch. Something about the scene below looked familiar, but I didn't think it was the blackened area.

We kept going after Jericho said we'd send Realm Two out to scout it later.

Two-hundred miles farther on, we saw another spot. This one was bigger than the last. Jericho exchanged a worried glance with Cairo, but called for us to continue onward.

When we had gone maybe another five-hundred miles, we spotted a third blackened area, even bigger.

At each spot, I had that weird itch at the back of my mind. I told Jericho we should check it out. We flew lower, but when we got close, I saw a weird rock formation nearby. It looked like three big boulders stacked together. That's when it hit me, what had been bugging me—I recognized this place. I realized I had seen the other places, too.

"Oh my gosh," I blurted, "I know what these are. I know these places."

"Where do you know these from?" Jericho's voice sounded tight with worry, and with good reason.

I told him, "These are some of the places where Eldrick sacrificed Trolls. I saw them in my visions. They were all over the earth. Farms, jungles, snow... Everywhere."

In his eyes, I didn't see the reassurance I had hoped for. Instead, his eyes grew wide and he said exactly what I had hoped he wouldn't. "The land is already dying. I didn't think he had killed enough to start it, but apparently he did."

My heart sank. I hadn't wanted to believe it, but when Jericho said it out loud, I knew it was true. "The Trolls he killed..."

He nodded. "They were enough to cause the environment to start deteriorating. If you don't find a way to reverse this, the Earth itself is going to be nothing more than a wasteland."

Cairo, sounding terrified, said, "By Aprella, this is the end of everything. Maybe we won the battle, but Eldrick is going to destroy everything anyway.

The world will be his, if we can't find out how to stop this."

Without looking, I reached out with one wingtip and grabbed Eva's. The day before had been just one small win in the bigger picture. We rushed back to Ochana as fast as we could go. I didn't know how much time we had to figure things out, but I knew we would all work as hard as we could to save the world—again.

J.A. Culican

Books by J.A. Culican

Novels

The Prince Returns-Keeper of Dragons book 1
The Elven Alliance-Keeper of Dragons book 2
The Mere Treaty-Keeper of Dragons book 3
The Crowns' Accord-Keeper of Dragons book 4
Second Sight-Hollows Ground book 1
Slayer-Dragon Tamer book 1
Warrior-Dragon Tamer book 2
Protector-Dragon Tamer book 3

Short Stories

The Golden Dragon-Keeper of Dragons short story
Jericho-Keeper of Dragons short story
Phoenix-Hollows Ground short story
Savior-Dragon Tamer short story

About the author

About J.A. Culican

J.A. Culican is a USA Today Bestselling author of the middle grade fantasy series Keeper of Dragons. Her first novel in the fictional series catapulted a trajectory of titles and awards, including top selling author on the USA Today bestsellers list and Amazon, and a rightfully earned spot as an international best seller. Additional accolades include Best Fantasy Book of 2016, Runner-up in Reality Bites Book Awards, and 1st place for Best Coming of Age Book from the Indie book Awards.

J.A. Culican holds a Master's degree in Special Education from Niagara University, in which she has been teaching special education for over 12 years. She is also the president of the autism awareness non-profit Puzzle Peace United. J.A. Culican resides in Southern New Jersey with her husband and four young children.

Contact me

I can't wait to hear from you!

Email:
jaculican@gmail.com

Website:
http://jaculican.com

Facebook Author Page:
 https://www.facebook.com/jaculican

Amazon Author Page:
http://amazon.com/author/jaculican

Twitter:
https://twitter.com/jaculican

Instagram:
http://instagram.com/jaculican

Pinterest:
http://pinterest.com/jaculican

Add me on Goodreads here:
https://www.goodreads.com/author/show/15287808.J_A_Culican

Made in the USA
Middletown, DE
12 July 2020

12581438R00175